BETWEEN WORLDS 4

WHAT FRIENDS DO

LORI WOLF-HEFFNER

HEAD IN THE GROUND PUBLISHING

CHAPTER ONE

The greasy smells of hamburgers and sausages greeted Juliana as she dropped her bag on the floor.

"Hey!" Dad looked up from the stove, a smile on his face. "How was your first day of the semester?"

Juliana couldn't answer. She swallowed but she could no longer hold in her tears.

"Jules?" He now looked concerned. "What's wrong?"

Emotions rose up in her but no words. She ran into her room and slammed the door behind her. She reached for her bag so she could call Rachel right away, and remembered she'd left it in the kitchen.

"Great," she muttered and swung her door to get it, almost crashing into Dad, who had followed her.

"You need to tell me what's wrong."

Where would she start? With the fact that moving in the middle of grade nine was the worst thing that had ever happened to her? That she sucked at her new dance studio? That life had been just fine back in Calgary? Or would she start with today's news and work her way back?

"Rachel's mom is on life support," she blurted out, choosing the last option.

Dad's eyes got big and his jaw dropped. "Kim? What happened?"

"Car accident and that's all I know. Now let me get my phone."

Dad stepped out of the way and followed Juliana back to the kitchen. "Jules, I'm so sorry."

Juliana whipped around to face him. "I could be there with her right now if we hadn't moved to Kitchener!" she yelled. She found her bag in the kitchen, stomped back to her room and slammed the door again.

She dialled Rachel's number, but no one answered, so she texted in case Rachel could see her phone but couldn't pick up.

Any news?

Dad knocked and came in. He pressed the heels of his hands to his eyes, took a deep breath, and then sat down in Juliana's office chair. "Listen, I know you're angry."

"You have no idea what I'm feel—"

Dad held up his hand. "Jules, just listen to me. I've

watched bad things happen to friends of mine, too. I can help you through this."

Juliana looked up. Why did he have to bring that up now? She was as mad as a tiger and he raised the one topic that could cut through that: his past, something he rarely spoke about.

Dad continued. "I know it's a horrible feeling when you can't be there to help your friends. But getting angry at me isn't going to help. Come have a snack. You know how you get when you're hungry. Then text Rachel."

Juliana wiped her eyes. "I already did. No answer."

Juliana could tell Dad wanted to hug her but was holding back. She wanted to hug him, too, but she was still pissed off that he and Mom had forced her to move halfway across the country. It had already been six weeks since they had moved and things hadn't improved. And now this with Rachel's mom.

"I have to flip the meat. Come out and eat something, even if it's something small. She'll respond when she's able to. Besides, you still have your homework to do, and dance tonight."

"I know that!" Her best friend's mom was on life support and all he could think about was her schedule?

Dad stepped into the hallway and waved for her to follow him. "Whatever happens, you need to take care of yourself. Trust me: it's the only way to get through these things and to be there for the person when they need you."

"FIVE, SIX, SEVEN, EIGHT!" MISS DENISE YELLED, AND ALL twenty-four dancers in Juliana's class began a series of flaps into a new formation while Miss Denise clapped out the beat. Their first competition was in a few weeks so every class they practised different sections of the dance.

Juliana arrived at her spot, threw her arm up, her fist exploding into a jazz hand, and immediately ducked as she saw someone else's hand coming at her. She realized she had used her left hand when she should have thrown up her right. Miss Denise stopped and sighed.

"Okay. Let's try again."

"Sorry," Juliana mumbled and she dragged her feet to her starting position.

"Five, six, seven, eight!"

Juliana started her flaps.

Rachel had finally texted. She was with her dad. No change in her mom. She wished Juliana was there with her.

Juliana hadn't known what to say so she had replied, "Text me as soon as you need something." Was that cold? But what else could she do from across the country?

"Juliana!" Miss Denise called out.

Everyone stared at Juliana, and she shrank under their frustration and impatience.

"You're in my spot," Mackenzie said, pushing a purple strip of hair out of her eyes.

Juliana mumbled another apology and trudged back to her starting position. Out of the corner of her eye, she caught a look of concern from Jasmine, the best dancer in the group.

"Juliana," Miss Denise said, her tone softer now. "You seem really distracted. Is everything okay?"

Juliana nodded.

"Are you sure?" Miss Denise asked.

Juliana glanced around at the class again. Jasmine looked skeptical but everyone else looked annoyed, obviously wanting to get on with practice.

"Yeah, I'm fine."

"Okay. Then let's take it from the top."

This time, Juliana got the arms right and landed in the right position, but when it came to the kick, she had to jerk her foot back before she broke Mackenzie's nose.

Miss Denise clapped to signal everyone should stop.

Juliana crossed her arms and looked down at the floor. "Sorry, everyone."

Jasmine touched her shoulder. "You're usually more focused than this. Something must be really bothering you. Whatever it is, we're here for you."

A few of the dancers nodded in agreement with Jasmine and the tension in the studio relaxed.

Juliana looked up. "Rachel, my best friend from Calgary? Her mom's on life support." Tears formed in Juliana's eyes.

Murmurs of concern rippled through the team and two girls gave Juliana a quick rub on the shoulder.

"I'm sorry to hear that," Miss Denise said. "Do you need to take five? Get a drink of water or something?"

Juliana nodded. Her arms still crossed, shoulders hunched over, chin down to hide her face, she walked out of the studio, down the long corridor, and into the junior girls' dressing room. She zipped open her bag and pulled her phone from its usual pouch.

Nothing more from Rachel. "Maybe she doesn't need me," Juliana whispered but she stared at her phone for the full five minutes, hoping a new message would come through.

IT WAS LATE WHEN RACHEL FINALLY CALLED.

"Juliana, it's awful. Mom's got all these tubes attached to her..." She broke off, sobbing.

Juliana didn't know what to say. She opened the photos on her phone. Scrolling through pictures, she noticed Kim's spunky haircuts and pink highlights in one picture, her round face smiling at something funny Juliana or Rachel had said in another. She had taken a picture of Kim scowling at the mess in Rachel's room. This was how Juliana wanted to think of Rachel's mom, not tied up to tubes like she was in some medical show.

Rachel sniffled. "Her face is all bruised and swollen, and she's got an oxygen mask on. I can barely look at her."

"Rach…" Juliana was crying now, too.

There was a knock on Juliana's door, and Mom popped her head in. Juliana had told her on the way home from the studio what had happened. "Don't stay up too late," she whispered. Juliana nodded. Mom gave a thumbs-up and a thumbs-down signal, asking how Kim was, and Juliana replied with a thumbs-down. Mom placed her hand on her heart.

"Mom's really sad for you guys," Juliana said. "She said she hopes your mom comes home soon."

Mom nodded and then bowed out of Juliana's room, softly closing the door behind her.

"Oh. That's nice of her. Thank you."

Juliana let out a little laugh.

"What?" Rachel asked.

"You remember the tattoo situation, right?"

"We got in a lot of trouble because of that. What's so funny about it?"

"The week after. When we coloured our hair purple? I've got that picture up on my phone right now," Juliana explained.

Juliana heard Rachel laugh softly, and it relieved her.

"The one where you can see all the dye on our foreheads?"

"Yup." Juliana laughed at the memory. "It was the first

time I finally understood why your mom paid a hundred dollars every time she wanted to get her hair highlighted."

Rachel laughed again. It felt good to laugh for a few moments.

"Wait..." Rachel said. "Remember how she invented and made us that triple-layer strawberry trifle when we got it all scrubbed off?"

"With extra whipping cream and chocolate chips."

"She makes it all the time now." Rachel paused, and Juliana heard more sniffles. "But she's never written the recipe down."

Another pause. Kim was a great cook. *Unlike Mom*, Juliana thought. It was something Juliana could never figure out: both Mom and Kim worked in grocery stores, and yet Kim could cook spectacular meals and Mom's were just okay.

"Rach? What if you tried to make her a trifle and then took it the hospital? Don't they say smells are really powerful?"

Another pause, and this time, Juliana sensed it wasn't a good one. When Rachel finally spoke, Juliana heard a sting in her voice. "Seriously? That's your suggestion? To waste time baking something I don't know how to bake and then take it to my mom, who's tied up to more tubes than I can count, and pretend like it's some kind of stupid Christmas movie?"

Juliana was silent.

"Really, Jules, you're not helping."

Juliana's cheeks burned, though it wasn't only from embarrassment. She was trying her best. But she remembered the promise she had made to herself at lunchtime when Rachel had first called with the news: she wasn't going to dump her own stuff on Rachel; she was going to support her.

"I'm sorry," she said meekly.

CHAPTER TWO

Elisabeth stepped out of the small shop with her wares: salt for cooking, and nails for Mammi to make shoes. Although piles of crystallized snow still remained, much of it had melted, making for a very muddy walk on the dirt roads in her village. The smell of spring hung in the air. Elisabeth adjusted her headscarf to protect her ears from the cool wind but she couldn't wait for the warmer weather when she wouldn't need to wear it outside anymore.

As she walked back to her house, she saw her cousin Georg Schuhmacher and his friend, Stefan Schäfer, walking toward her.

"Good day, Lissika," Stefan said, a sunny smile on his face.

"Good day, Stefan, Georg," she replied, trying not to

focus on Stefan's missing arm. Stefan had returned from a prisoner-of-war camp in Russia the month before and although Elisabeth had already spoken with him on several occasions, her eyes darted every time to the empty air next to his body where an arm should have been hanging.

Georg merely nodded as he blew out smoke from a cigarette. Ever since he had returned a year ago from the great war that had almost swallowed Europe, Georg rarely spoke to anyone and often succumbed to incoherent screaming and fits where he would see things no one else could.

"We're getting some supplies for Georg's workshop," Stefan said. Georg and his father were two of the few blacksmiths in Semlak, their tiny Romanian village.

"I just returned from shopping," Elisabeth replied. "And now I have to go study. I have my confirmation on Palm Sunday."

Stefan tipped his hat to her. "May God help you!" he said cheerfully.

Georg said nothing but gave a curt nod, normally an insulting snub, but Elisabeth had come to learn that, for Georg, it was a friendly goodbye.

Elisabeth grumbled to herself about Mammi's mood: she had just taken the nails to her and hadn't received even a thank you. She wiped her boots on the mat outside the house, stepped through the house door and into the kitchen, where she placed the small bag of salt on the loam-and-chaff floor, and used a cloth to remove the rest of the mud from her boots. The kitchen was the middle room of their simple three-room home and had the only door to outside. To the left of the kitchen, with windows facing to the street, was the front room, where the family slept, entertained close friends and family, and spent time with one another. To the right of the kitchen was the back room, which was used for formal visits and guests who needed to stay the night. Over the doorway in each room hung a crucifix.

Rosina, Elisabeth's youngest sibling, ran out of the front room. "This is you!" she declared, showing Elisabeth a dried cob of corn, cut in half. She thrust another half in Elisabeth's face. "And this is Mammi!"

"Do I really look like that?" Elisabeth slipped into her house shoes. Rosina had chosen the stubby bottom half of the corn to represent Elisabeth.

"No, but Mammi looks like this one, so you have to be the other one. Anna has the ones for Luki and Tata, and then our dolls are me and her."

"Rosina!" Anna called out from the front room. "Tata's about to leave for America. Come on! Everyone has to say goodbye!" Rosina darted back into the front room to reenact their father's departure in November with the dolls.

"It'll soon be time for your handiwork!" Elisabeth shouted after Rosina, but no one answered.

As Elisabeth folded her shawl and carried it and her knitted mittens to the back room, she couldn't help but be concerned that Rosina had chosen the skinnier corn cob for Mammi. It was a fitting choice because Mammi had been very sick and was becoming skinnier. She had told Elisabeth why—she was having a baby—and sworn her to secrecy. Elisabeth had looked it up in Tata's encyclopedia to understand better. It explained that the baby would be born in either ten lunar or nine solar months. If the baby came earlier, when it wasn't fully developed, it was called either a miscarriage or a premature birth. The encyclopedia listed complaints that came with expecting a baby, including a lack of appetite, nausea, and vomiting—exactly what Mammi had been experiencing for several weeks at least. But when the encyclopedia had begun describing a mother's shame area, Elisabeth had slammed the book shut. She knew there were some things she was too young to learn about.

She was not too young to know that Mammi wasn't supposed to be getting skinnier, but whenever Elisabeth tried to convince Mammi to get help, Mammi got angry at her and threatened to force her to kneel in the box of dried corn kernels that was kept in the kitchen for severe punishments. Elisabeth was at a loss to know what to do. But if Mammi didn't get fat again, would she have a miscarriage?

Elisabeth shook the worries out of her mind: they weren't helping. She had time before supper preparation, so she sat in the back room to study Martin Luther's *Small Catechism*, which she had to memorize in time for her confirmation on Palm Sunday, only a few weeks away. With confirmation, she and several others her age would become adults in the church and finally be allowed to dance with boys, although she would have to wait until after Easter. There were no dances during Lent.

Elisabeth pulled a blanket around her shoulders. The brick-and-lime oven in the kitchen protruded into the front room, heating it comfortably, but the back room had no source of heat. Still, she liked studying there as it allowed her to get away from her siblings. She opened up the catechism to find the Lord's Prayer, her favourite prayer:

Our Father, who art in Heaven,

Hallowed be Thy name.

Thy kingdom come,

Thy will be done on Earth as it is in Heaven.

Give us this day our daily bread,

and forgive us our trespasses as we forgive those who trespass against us.

And lead us not into temptation, but deliver us from evil.

Amen.

Although she had memorized much over the last two years, she still had a good amount to learn over the next few weeks. Elisabeth loved to read, and Tata had always encouraged it and taught her in the evenings from the family's encyclopedia and Martin Luther's writings. But with Tata away in America to earn money for the family, Mammi had demanded Elisabeth care for the household and her siblings so that Mammi could run Tata's shoe-making shop behind the family home.

Elisabeth glanced up at the crucifix. *Thank you for this time*, she said to Jesus and then returned her attention to her book. Luther had broken up his lessons on the Lord's Prayer by petition. She understood the first two: "Hallowed be Thy name" and "Thy kingdom come." The third one was more complicated: "Thy will be done on Earth as it is in Heaven." About it, Luther wrote:

What does this mean?

Answer: The good and gracious will of God is indeed done without our prayer; but we pray in this petition that it may be done among us also.

How is this done?

Answer: When God breaks and hinders every evil counsel and will which would not let us hallow God's name nor let His kingdom come, such as the will of the Devil, the world, and our flesh, but strengthens and preserves us steadfast in His Word and faith unto our end. This is His gracious and good will.

Elisabeth re-read the text three more times, and each time it made less sense than the time before. She glanced up at the cross and silently asked Jesus for help. Unfortunately, none came. *He's probably looking after another family today*, she thought. She memorized the page number, closed the book, and headed into the kitchen to make Mammi a snack, hoping Mammi could eat it.

After spreading butter on bread and sprinkling it with paprika to help Mammi's stomach, Elisabeth laced up her boots and headed out along the side of the house, past the attached cellar, and into the summer kitchen where Tata had built his workshop. Several gas lanterns on the workbench provided light and a tiny bit of warmth for Mammi; the workshop had no oven or stove to provide heat.

Mammi sat hunched over Tata's worn and scratched work bench, the edges of her white bonnet—her *haube*—sticking out from under her dark blue headscarf. Several shawls hung around her shoulders and settled on her lap. Mammi tapped one of the nails Elisabeth had just bought into the heel of a shoe.

"What now?" Mammi asked without looking up.

"I brought you something to eat, and I have a question about my studies."

Elisabeth didn't smell vomit, so either Mammi had kept

down the bit of lunch she'd eaten or she had dumped out the bowl herself.

"I'm busy, Lissika, so hurry up."

Elisabeth opened the book and read the passage she didn't understand. "I've tried re-reading it, but I'm not sure what Martin Luther means."

Mammi didn't look up from her work. "Then you're not studying hard enough. Now leave me alone."

Elisabeth closed the book and sighed. Mammi's mood had become almost intolerable. She had rarely shown the children any patience even when Tata was home but after he had left, she had had less patience and, since this sickness had come upon her, none.

Without saying a word, Elisabeth left her mother and returned to the house.

After reviewing the passage more, she gave up. Maybe Jesus would give her an answer at night. She read the remaining petitions of the Lord's Prayer, realizing with relief that she understood the rest. She still had to commit them to memory, but she didn't feel like it right now. *I'll do it while I'm ironing tomorrow*, she thought and skipped ahead to the sacrament of baptism, the last bit she wanted to read before preparing supper.

Who would the baby's godparents be? Elisabeth thought as she studied Luther's words. She would only find that out after the baby was born, but after reading the encyclopedia entry, and knowing that many mothers lost babies, Elisabeth worried again. Mammi had already lost children before, including Anna's twin sister, who had died at birth. What if Mammi continued to be sick? Her face was growing thinner and paler by the day. Elisabeth tried to shake the frightening thoughts away, but her mind kept returning to them. Mammi needed help.

"I'll call the midwife," Elisabeth finally decided. "If the midwife says Mammi's healthy, then I'll feel better. And if she's not, then Mammi will have to do something about it and I'll know what it is."

THE NEXT DAY, ONCE ANNA AND LUKI WERE OFF TO SCHOOL and Rosina had gone to a friend's house, Elisabeth had run out quickly to call on one of the midwives in the village. Now, she waited impatiently in the kitchen, with a few *lei* for payment on the table, while the midwife met with Mammi in the front room. Elisabeth had Luther's *Small Catechism* open again on the table, but instead of memorizing the petitions of the Lord's Prayer, she thought about the questions running through her head: would Tata come home for the baby's birth? What if Mammi died when the baby tried to come out? Or what if the baby died? If the baby lived, would Elisabeth have to look after it, too? She didn't know how to look after a baby.

Elisabeth had to stop thinking about the questions. She

put the book away and began to do her ironing. She tried to listen in on the conversation, but Mammi and the midwife spoke in hushed tones.

Finally, the door opened, startling Elisabeth, and the midwife invited her in. Elisabeth set the iron on the stove and followed her. Judging by the look on Mammi's face, the news wasn't good.

"Your mother will say differently, Elisabeth, but you were right to call me."

Elisabeth twisted her hands. No matter the outcome of this conversation, it would not end well for her. "Is she all right?"

To her relief, the midwife nodded and Elisabeth breathed out. "She will be fine," the midwife explained, "but she must rest more. She's been working too hard."

"I have too much to do, Frau Molnár," Mammi stated. "We are not dripping in money. The baby will come soon, so I must earn as much as I can."

"Frau Schuhmacher, I would not call three or four months soon."

Three or four months? That was when the baby would come? Elisabeth's mind began to whirl again.

"It is soon enough."

"Regardless, you are too far into your condition to be getting sick. You must rest."

Mammi stood up and smoothed out her dress and work apron. "I am fine," she insisted.

The midwife reached behind her waist to untie her own apron. "How old are you, Frau Schuhmacher?"

Mammi's face turned dark. "Thirty-four. Why?"

"That confirms my suspicion. You're too old to have children anymore. You've already lost two babies. Do not make this a third one." The midwife folded her apron into her bag. "You do not have to stop working, but you must rest during the day. Your husband's drafty, damp workshop is no place for a woman in your condition in this weather." She closed up her bag and headed into the kitchen and to the house door. Elisabeth retrieved her coat from the back room and handed it to her.

"I will say it one more time," Frau Molnár said. "You must rest at least once every day, more if possible." She looked Elisabeth directly in the eye. "Your mother says you are in charge of the household now." Elisabeth nodded. "Do what you can to ensure your mother rests. Good day." The midwife took the payment Elisabeth handed her and then left.

No sooner had the door closed behind her than Mammi said, "That woman has no idea what she's talking about." She glared at Elisabeth. "Do not ever embarrass me like that again or waste our money on something so useless." She slipped into her boots. "Get me my shawls."

Elisabeth knew better than to argue: right now she was thankful Mammi had not punished her. She obeyed her mother, who grabbed the shawls out of Elisabeth's hands and headed out to the workshop without another word.

"Did I make the wrong choice?" she asked Jesus on the cross in the kitchen. "Should I have obeyed Mammi? Have I dishonoured her by not listening, even though the midwife said I'd made the right choice?"

Elisabeth's studies included memorizing the Ten Commandments and Martin Luther's interpretation of them. She found most of the commandments easy to follow—"Thou shalt have no other gods before me," "Thou shalt not kill," and "Thou shalt sanctify the holy day." But the fourth commandment caused her frequent problems, and she frequently prayed to Jesus for help with it: "Thou shalt honour thy father and thy mother, that it may be well with thee, and thou mayest live long on the earth."

At Christmas when Mammi had told Elisabeth about the changes in the household, Elisabeth had found strength in the fourth commandment to make it through. However, earlier this year, when she had discovered that Tata had written his first letter from America to his brother and not to Mammi, and that he had even asked Konrad-Bátschi not to tell Mammi because he hadn't found a good job yet, Elisabeth didn't know which parent to obey. She wanted to honour Tata's request, but she knew how worried Mammi had been, not knowing whether Tata had arrived safely in America.

Mammi had eventually directed Elisabeth to obey her,

because she was here and Tata was not. That made sense to Elisabeth. But now, Mammi was here and was ignoring the midwife's orders. Tata would want to see his new baby, even if he couldn't be here for its birth. Was Elisabeth to obey Mammi because she was here or Tata because he would like to see his fifth child?

Elisabeth continued ironing. "She's being stubborn again, sticking to her ways, even when it doesn't help anyone," she said to herself. Elisabeth pressed down harder on the iron, not knowing what else to do with her frustration. She recited the Lord's Prayer, hoping it would somehow give her an answer.

CHAPTER THREE

"For your homework, you had to think about where you live," Ms. Haseltine said. "What gives you a sense of place? Something about the landscape? Or your home in particular? Something about the people?"

Juliana peeked at her phone. Still nothing from Rachel.

As far as Juliana was concerned, other than Shawna and Meghan, this geography class was a group of strangers. She had begun at Eby Heights just after Christmas break, attended classes for a few weeks, written three exams, and now was starting the new semester with a new class.

Meghan had asked Juliana to join her and Shawna for a group assignment during last semester's phys ed class and they'd eaten lunch together ever since, sometimes just the three of them, sometimes with other friends of the two girls. But in this class, they were the only two people Juliana knew.

She peeked at her phone again.

"Juliana?" Ms. Haseltine said. "Your phone should be off."

Embarrassed at having been called out, Juliana's head sank into her shoulders. But she hadn't heard anything from Rachel all morning. *Maybe her mom has woken up and Rachel's talking with her*, she thought and tried to comfort herself with that sliver of hope.

Ms. Haseltine pointed to a boy who had raised his hand to share his homework with the class. He read from his paper. "My apartment is special. We're on the nineteenth floor, and we can see lots of trees from our balcony." He stopped.

Ms. Haseltine waited then said, "Is that it?"

The boy shrugged. "I couldn't think of anything else."

A few students snickered. Ms. Haseltine didn't stop them, leading Juliana to assume she expected no more from this boy.

"I had hockey practice," the boy said, a hint of defiance in his voice.

Juliana snorted. Several students looked in her direction, and her cheeks turned red. She'd had dance practice, had practised at home, too, completed her homework for her other classes, had a best friend whose mom was in intensive care on the other side of the country, and she had still managed to write a full-page answer for the assignment.

"What?" the boy said. "I'll earn millions once I'm drafted. Who needs this?"

Ms. Haseltine's answer surprised Juliana; it wasn't a typical 'teacher' response. "When you're a big name in hockey, Alex, one of the things you'll get asked is what your hometown was like. If you don't have a good answer, you'll insult everyone here who ever supported you. And chances are you're going to lose PR points because you didn't bother to think about what makes K-W special to you."

K-W was short for Kitchener-Waterloo, Juliana's new city. Actually Kitchener and Waterloo were two separate cities, but most people here treated them almost as one: only large, green signs told you there was even a border.

Alex's jaw dropped. He obviously hadn't thought of that. Juliana tried not to smirk. She checked her phone again.

"Juliana, why don't you give us your answer? Class is obviously boring you."

Juliana snapped her head to the front. "I'm...I'm sorry," she stammered.

"Do I need to remind you about the cell phone policy at this school?"

Juliana shook her head. She could see Meghan's expression out of the corner of her eye; she knew why Juliana was constantly checking her phone.

"What's your answer?"

Juliana looked down at her neatly typed assignment. "All of it?"

Ms. Haseltine peered over Juliana's binder. "Maybe just the first paragraph."

"I've lost my sense of place," Juliana began. No sooner had she read those words than her eyes welled up with tears. Quickly, she blinked them back and arranged her ruler under the first line to help her track where she was. "Back home in Calgary, I could see the Rockies on a clear day. And although I'm not a sports fan, seeing the Saddledome whenever I went downtown filled me with pride. When I go to downtown Kitchener, everything looks messy."

"Hey!" Alex said.

Juliana shot him a look and Ms. Haseltine shushed him. "Continue," she said to Juliana.

Juliana swallowed again: a lump in her throat was growing. "I have friends there. And we did a lot of things together. I'm meeting nice people here—" She gave a weak smile to Meghan and Shawna—"but it takes a long time to make really good friends. I used to go to dance competitions with those friends. Sometimes we'd drive up to Edmonton where the land got flatter, and sometimes we'd drive over the border to Montana where we'd get closer to the mountains. I haven't crossed the border here, but my father has. He's a truck driver. He says it's way different on this side of the continent. But when he tells me about it, I miss the stories he has about driving through the Rockies."

Juliana took a deep breath. *Tears, go away*, she thought. She looked up at her teacher. Ms. Haseltine was probably one of the youngest teachers at the school, and with her outdoorsy style of dress, she could have come from Alberta herself.

"So you miss home," Ms. Haseltine said.

Juliana nodded, afraid to open her mouth. The lump in her throat had grown into a stone, ready to catapult itself out and release her tears if she spoke. Ms. Haseltine eyed her for a moment, and then, to Juliana's relief, she moved on to another student.

Juliana checked her phone again. Still nothing. She so wanted to text Rachel and tell her how maddening this distance was between the two of them, but she reminded herself of her promise. No matter how hard it was going to be, Juliana would not complain to Rachel about her own problems.

MOM WAS HOME WHEN JULIANA GOT IN THE DOOR. HER schedule at the grocery store she managed changed every week, and sometimes she got called in when there was an emergency (although Juliana couldn't figure out what would be so important that employees and assistant managers couldn't handle things on their own). It meant Juliana never really knew when her mom would be home. That was why Dad had cooked so much before he had left for another long-haul trip: Juliana could grab a container from the freezer and nuke it for her and her grandfather if needed.

"How are you feeling?" Mom asked.

Juliana dropped her bag on a chair in the kitchen. "Horrible."

"Apple? Almonds?"

"And water." Then she added, "Please." Juliana appreciated that Mom was trying to be helpful. "I did okay in my assignment for geography."

"Well, I guess that's one good thing, isn't it?"

Juliana shrugged. Mom set her plate down in front of her, and Juliana yawned while she picked at the food.

"I'm guessing you were up late last night?" Mom asked.

"Yeah. But Rachel hasn't texted me all day."

"She probably needs to be with her family right now. I know this may be hard for you to hear, but she does have other people to help her."

Juliana shot Mom an angry look. "I know she has other friends, but I'm her best friend! I should be there for her and instead I'm stuck here in this gross, gray city halfway across the world."

Mom gave Juliana the 'Really?' look. "You're separated

only by a few thousand kilometres, not half the world. You have your phone—"

"Well, she's not answering!"

"Because she has a lot to process," Mom said calmly. "Whatever happens, you're going to need energy for her, your schooling, and your dance. Eat."

Exactly what Dad had said. Juliana nibbled on an almond. But where was Rachel? She pulled out her phone to check. Still nothing.

"Why won't she text?" Juliana said. She popped a few almonds into her mouth.

Mom stroked Juliana's long hair. "She's going through a really tough time. You have to realize, you're over here now. You have to—"

Juliana jerked her head to shake off Mom's hand. "I know where I am," she said. "And I can't be the best friend I want to be for Rachel because you dragged me here."

Now anger clouded Mom's face, too. "That's not fair," she said. "Do you really expect me to leave my father as he is? Forgetting things? Not knowing sometimes if he's here or back home in Romania? You've already seen his blips, Juliana. They're going to get worse. If your dad were in trouble, would you stay wherever you were on the slim chance that tragedy could hit your best friend? Or would you move to look after your father, who raised you and gave you the life you have?"

"I'd stay near those who cared about me!" No sooner

had the words escaped Juliana's mouth that she regretted them. They were harsh, even for a fight with her mom. But it was how she felt sometimes, with her parents too often at work, and when they were home, too often arguing with her rather than understanding.

Mom's mouth dropped open, but before she could say anything, Juliana's phone rang: it was Rachel.

"Oh my god, Rach, what's going on? How are you doing? How's your mom?"

But Rachel was crying so hard that she couldn't get words out of her mouth. Tears already began to run down Juliana's cheeks. At that moment, Juliana's grandfather, Opa, came up the stairs and into the kitchen.

"Jules..." Rachel said, "she..." But she couldn't finish her sentence.

"She died?"

"Yes..."

Juliana's heart broke.

"I don't know...what...I'm going to do..." Rachel said between sobs.

Juliana didn't either.

"What's wrong?" Opa asked, but Mom shushed him.

Juliana's tears were dripping into her mouth. "I wish I could be there for you."

"So do I," Rachel said. After a few seconds of silence, Rachel said, "I have to go...I have to help Dad with funeral...stuff."

"Call me whenever you need me, okay, Rachel? Whenever. I don't care what time it is, okay? I'll have my phone with me everywhere I go, okay?"

"You're my best friend, Jules. Thanks."

"Best friends forever, just like we promised."

After Juliana hung up, she stood frozen in the kitchen. Now she understood what people meant when they said time stood still. She had lost all orientation of what day or time it was, what she had just done, what she was going to do next. Time had crashed to a stop.

"I'm so sorry," Mom said, her voice soft.

The anger Juliana had experienced when she and her parents had first moved here didn't compare to the anger that was welling up inside of her now.

"What happened?" Opa asked again.

Juliana's anger spilled out. "I never asked for any of this! All I ever wanted was to be with my friends in the city I grew up in. That's it! Nothing else!"

She grabbed her bag, ran to her bedroom, slammed the door behind her, and collapsed onto her bed in sobs.

CHAPTER FOUR

$\mathcal{E}$lisabeth dipped a small bowl into the ceramic wash basin, scooping up water, and began sprinkling it all over the kitchen floor to dampen it. The floors in all farmers' homes were made of compacted loam and chaff; dampening it reduced how much dust flew into the air from sweeping. Anna and Luki were long gone to school, so only Rosina was home.

"Rosina, sweep the kitchen," Elisabeth said.

"But I want to knit," Rosina replied. "I'm almost done my fourth row." Elisabeth wondered if all six-year-olds were this stubborn.

"Yes, you are getting faster, but you need to help around here, too." She dumped the rest of the water back into the wash basin.

Rosina pouted but grabbed the broom. Elisabeth filled

a mug with tea she had reheated on the stove for Mammi. In truth, she knew her mother probably didn't want tea, but Elisabeth needed an excuse to go see Mammi without awakening any suspicion in her youngest sister.

"I'll be right back," she said as she slipped into her boots, tucking the laces inside. Elisabeth ignored Rosina sticking her tongue out, and left.

"What?" Mammi grumbled as Elisabeth entered the workshop.

"I wanted to bring you some tea. It's still chilly out here."

"You came to tell me to take a rest. I am tired of repeating myself, Elisabeth. You are studying Luther's catechism. Tell me, what is the fourth commandment?"

Elisabeth recited from the catechism by heart: "'Thou shalt honour thy father and thy mother, that it may be well with thee, and thou mayest live long on the earth.'"

"And what does it mean?"

Elisabeth took a deep breath and quoted again. "'We should fear and love God that we may not despise our parents and masters, nor provoke them to anger, but give them honour, serve and obey them, and hold them in love and esteem.'"

Although Elisabeth was proud she had said those words without a mistake, Mammi did not pay her any compliments.

"You are provoking me to anger, which means you do

not fear and love God as you should," Mammi said. "So follow what you are studying and leave me alone."

Elisabeth sighed, set down the tea, and left. Once outside, she leaned against the white wall of the house. "Jesus, none of this makes sense to me," she said out loud. "Am I to obey my parents when I know what they're asking me to do isn't the best choice?" She reviewed to herself Luther's final comments on the Ten Commandments: "God threatens to punish all that transgress these commandments. Therefore we should fear His wrath, and not act contrary to them. But He promises grace and every blessing to all that keep these commandments. Therefore we should also love and trust in Him, and willingly do according to His commandments."

Elisabeth looked up at the sky. "Lord Jesus, I shouldn't be punished for disobeying my mother if it saves my new sibling, should I?" The Lord's Prayer came to mind. "You tell us that if we forgive others, God will forgive us. Would I be forgiven for disobeying Mammi, even though Martin Luther says we will be punished for not obeying Your father's commandments? Because if I listen to Mammi, the baby might die."

"HARD CURRENCY SPECULATORS SET FORTH THEIR TACTICS!" the postman called out to the crowd who had come to hear the news from the wider world. "Clever as they are, the speculators have recently spread the news that certain stamped banknotes were not good!"

He continued, "Customs Office announces that from now on, any person who crosses the border cannot have in his possession more than 2,000 *lei*!"

"Local hairdressing workers have asked their employers for salary raises!"

Having given the news to all assembled, the postman then handed out what mail he had, collected what was given to him, mounted his horse and headed on to the next town. The crowd began to disperse.

Elisabeth shook her head.

"What?" Rosina asked as she adjusted her headscarf.

"Borders. Not only do we live in a new country, even though we live in the same house, but we now have to cross a border to go home to Hungary."

Rosina furrowed her eyebrows. "What's a border?"

Elisabeth just waved her hand at her sister. She didn't want to answer such a complicated question right now. Rosina found a stone on the ground and began to kick it.

"Oh, don't do that," Elisabeth pleaded. "You'll scuff up your shoes."

Despite her sister's request, Rosina continued kicking at the stone. Elisabeth threw her hands in the air in frustration and wondered why God hadn't given Moses an eleventh commandment: honour thy siblings. She immediately apologized to God for her thoughts. Of course God would only do what was right. He was God, after all.

Elisabeth began to follow Rosina, occasionally pleading that her sister stop kicking the stone. The sound of wagon wheels and a horse's hooves drew her attention and she turned around to see Georg atop a horse pulling a wagon. In the wagon sat three men: Georg's brother, Samuel; his father, Tata's brother, Konrad-Bátschi; and Stefan.

"Elisabeth!" Samuel yelled at her, waving his hat.

"Go on ahead," Elisabeth said to Rosina. "I'll be home shortly."

Rosina nodded and continued following the stone as she kicked it.

"You'll be polishing those yourself!" Elisabeth shouted after her sister, but if Rosina heard her, she didn't show any sign of it.

"Lissika," Konrad-Bátschi said, his face consumed by its usual scowl. "Acting ladylike, I see."

Elisabeth refused to be drawn into an argument with her uncle: no matter what he said, it would be unreason-able. "I came out to hear the news," she said as cheerfully as she could. "How are all of you?" Her eyes darted to Stefan's missing arm and she quickly pulled her gaze away from it. *It's just an arm*, she admonished herself, only to catch herself staring at it again.

"Doing well," Samuel replied. Stefan's smile indicated

he was also well. She looked up at Georg, who simply nodded at her.

"Say something, you oaf!" Konrad-Bátschi said to his eldest son.

Georg looked in the other direction.

"You're as useless as a dead horse," Konrad-Bátschi said.

Stefan and Samuel looked away, too, out of embarrassment.

Elisabeth tried to change the subject. "Where are you off to?"

Stefan's face brightened up at her invisible offer to draw the unwanted attention away from his friend. "Samuel brought some tools to the workshop for Georg and Herr Schuhmacher to repair. Now we're all heading back to his *salasch* to start preparations for planting."

A *salasch* was a large piece of farmland just outside the village that had its own house but belonged to a family living in the village. Some families employed day labourers to live there and to care for the land, while others used the *salasch* as a second home for a married child and his or her family. Samuel and his wife, whose name was also Elisabeth, had moved to their family's *salasch* recently so they could take care of the land and start a family.

"Who will check your fields, Lissika?" Konrad-Bátschi asked. "Your father's left his family behind, and little Luki's too young for that kind of responsibility."

His accusation stung. Elisabeth knew her father and

uncle didn't get along. Much of it stemmed from Konrad-Bátschi's belief that Tata was jealous of him because, as the eldest brother, Konrad-Bátschi had inherited the black-smithing workshop. Elisabeth knew that Tata had never wanted the workshop, but that out of respect for their late father, he had never said so to his brother.

"Your mother should check the fields, but I've hardly seen her these past few weeks except for church." The look on his face suggested suspicion.

Elisabeth certainly wasn't going to divulge her mother's secret. She did her best to keep her composure, though Konrad-Bátschi was provoking anger inside her, the way one raises a wick in a lantern to intensify its flame. "Mammi is busy with shoes," Elisabeth said. It was not the full truth and Elisabeth promptly asked Jesus for forgiveness. "Thank you for your concern about our fields. I can check our vineyard but—"

"Elisabeth and I planned to go out tomorrow," Stefan said quickly.

"I planned to meet them there," Samuel added.

Not catching the cover-up, Konrad-Bátschi turned to Samuel. "When was this decided? You never said a word to me. You need to tend to our fields first!"

"It will just be an hour or two, Tata. Elisabeth—that is, my Elisabeth—can work alone for a couple of hours. Lissika needs help, they have less land than we do, and it's only kind that we help family."

Konrad-Bátschi grunted. "We're only helping her because my brother has deserted his family. No, Samuel, you're staying on our land and looking after it."

Georg snapped on the horse's reins to get going without warning. As the wagon's wheels began to roll, he spoke to Elisabeth in a monotone voice, "I'll be by tomorrow after breakfast to pick you up."

Konrad-Bátschi's neck bulged out and his face turned red. Elisabeth did all she could to hide her astonishment: Georg sometimes surprised her.

"Until tomorrow!" she called out to her cousins and their friend. Samuel and Stefan tipped their hats to her as the horse walked away, the gravel road and old snow crackling under the wagon wheels. Elisabeth scanned the area for Rosina and found her far down the road, toward home, still playing with her stone. Elisabeth ran to catch up with her.

"Rosina, look at your shoes!" Elisabeth scolded. "They're all scuffed! I told you not to play with that stone!"

"You'll polish them when we get home," Rosina said matter-of-factly.

"Looks like you'll be learning how to do that today," Elisabeth replied. "Let's go."

Before the girls turned on to their own road, Elisabeth heard a voice call her name. It was the dearest voice in the world, that of Maria, her best friend, who was now running toward the sisters.

"I'm so glad I found you!" Maria said, trying to catch her breath. "I wanted to get out to the postman and to see you, but then my mother needed help in the house. I was worried I'd missed you!"

Elisabeth smiled as the two girls kissed each other on each cheek. She sent Rosina home and told her to leave her boots on a mat in the front room. Rosina skipped off.

"I don't have much to tell you right now," Maria said, "but I am going to tease you for a moment!" She clapped her hands and did a little jump. "I'll come by to show you something sometime soon, maybe on Sunday after church. My grandmother's cousin who's also in Harrisburg, like your father, sent me a magazine. You have to see the fashion in America!"

Elisabeth's eyes opened wide. "From America?" She could barely contain her excitement: she had never seen anything from America before! Maria grabbed her hands and gave Elisabeth the biggest smile she had seen in a long time.

"They are so beautiful, Elisabeth. But listen to this: some women there wear pants!"

"Pants?"

"Yes! I'd tell you more now—" Though judging by Maria's playful expression, Elisabeth knew that wasn't true —"but I have to run errands for Mammi, and I know you have lots of work to do during the day. You're so good to your mother."

Elisabeth smiled as she let go of Maria's hands. "I can't wait!"

As Maria ran off, she shouted back to Elisabeth, "Oh! And I have another surprise for you! But you'll have to wait until Sunday!"

"That's unfair!" Elisabeth called back playfully.

In response, Maria turned fully to Elisabeth, did another little jump, then continued on her way.

Elisabeth could always count on Maria to lift her spirits, like when Elisabeth's family had been so very ill in January, especially Luki, and Maria had come by twice with soup. But now a surprise? It was only Thursday. How was Elisabeth going to handle this much excitement until Sunday?

So much joy flowed through Elisabeth that she forgot about her uncle's comments. A grin on her face, she picked up her skirt and ran home.

"That's all there is to it," Elisabeth said to Rosina as she finished polishing her baby sister's boots. "See? Nice and easy." She turned each one around in her hand. *You did a fine job, Lissika, if I do say so myself,* she thought. She still hadn't come down from the excitement of Maria's words.

"Thank you!" Rosina said and darted to her knitting basket.

Thank you? Elisabeth thought. *She's thanking me for showing her how to polish...oh.* Elisabeth realized that Rosina had somehow tricked her into polishing both boots for her. Her happiness slightly deflated, she sighed and let Rosina win this one. She carried the boots to the house door and began lunch preparations: pickles from last year's harvest, sliced salami from the last slaughter, and bread she had baked yesterday. On Mammi's bread she sprinkled paprika as usual. She called Rosina to the table and then took Mammi's food out to the workshop.

"Mammi?" she said as she carefully opened the door. The air reeked of vomit again. "I'll take that out for you," she said, reaching for the bowl Mammi used.

"I'm not hungry," Mammi said, still focused on her work.

Elisabeth set the plate of food down. "You have to eat. The midwife said—"

Mammi banged her fist on the table. "I know what the midwife said! She's a stupid cow. Obviously I can't stop working."

"You don't have to stop, just slow down. Please, Mammi."

Mammi didn't say a word, meaning the conversation was over. The daylight that shone in through the half-open door highlighted the thinness of Mammi's face.

"If you keep up like this," Elisabeth said, "the wind will blow you away."

"That's for little children, and you know that."

But that's how you're acting, Elisabeth thought. She knew that many women died when they had a baby. But if that happened to Mammi because she hadn't listened to the midwife...? Did Jesus punish women for not listening to midwives?

Elisabeth took the bowl of vomit and carried it across the wide yard to the manure pile. At the well, she pulled up a bucket of water and rinsed out the bowl, dumping the rinsing water onto the ground. She returned the bowl to Mammi, who, to Elisabeth's dismay, hadn't touched her plate.

"What if this baby isn't born because you're not listening to the midwife?" Elisabeth asked.

"God decides if a baby will be born. The midwife only knows how to get the baby out. Now, obey the fourth commandment and leave me alone."

Elisabeth realized that she believed more in the midwife's instructions than Mammi's. How could she get through to her mother? What would Tata tell her to do? *Tata!*

"Don't you want Tata to be able to see the baby?" Elisabeth asked. Mammi's hands stopped, and Elisabeth knew she had her attention. "What would Tata say if he found out the baby had died because you worked too hard?" Although the expression on Mammi's face didn't change, the fact that she had stopped working told Elisabeth she was considering it. Elisabeth pressed on. "Tata would feel very guilty. And the fourth commandment says to honour my parents. If I'm to obey Martin Luther's and God's words, I cannot lie to my father and not tell him that you didn't listen to the midwife."

After a few moments, Mammi sighed a heavy sigh and said, "You are more stubborn than a mule, Lissika." She set her hammer and the shoe down. "But you are right. I'll lie down for a little. But it means I will be working after supper, so you will need to take care of the mending tonight by yourself."

"Of course," Elisabeth replied, trying desperately to not jump up and down in excitement as Maria had.

Mammi pointed a finger at her. "Do not say a word to anyone. I do not need to be the topic of rumours at church on Sunday."

Elisabeth understood what Mammi meant: if people knew she was resting during the day, they would call her lazy. No self-respecting German would do anything to earn that name. Elisabeth promised she wouldn't and returned to the house. But the conversation left two unanswered questions: had she disobeyed the fourth commandment by speaking against Mammi? Or had she obeyed it in the end because Mammi had agreed with her?

She entered the house and found the pickle jar tipped over, pickles rolling all over the table, and pickle juice soaking into the clay-and-chaff floor.

"Rosina!" Elisabeth shouted.

"I'm knitting!"

Elisabeth sighed and leaned against the door. Whatever her moral dilemmas, she had more pressing matters to tend to right now.

"But at least Mammi will begin to rest," she said. "Thank you, Jesus, for helping me."

CHAPTER FIVE

Juliana stared at the next drawing in Omama's book: a lantern.

"Why was this so important to draw?" Juliana asked herself. Unfortunately, the drawing had no people or other objects to give her any hints about its context or purpose. "Maybe she was just practising."

She paged ahead to a drawing of a man in a coffin, although the coffin was very plain and thin, very different from the coffins Juliana occasionally saw on television. A sign stood next to it: it was shaped like a two-dimensional house, the kind a child draws, with a very long stake protruding from its base, probably so this sign could stick in the ground. Scribbles suggested words, but Omama hadn't filled them in. The man's hands were folded in prayer, and on his legs sat a large bouquet of flowers. Behind him stood nine people, their hands also folded in prayer. She and Dad had discovered this drawing shortly after Christmas, when they had paged through the book together, and it was the first drawing Juliana had come across that was of death. *How appropriate*, she thought, thinking of Rachel's mother.

"May I join you?"

It was Opa, standing in one of the two doorways that led into his home's small living room. He wore brown trousers, a black v-neck sweater, and brown slippers.

She nodded and he came and joined her on his ancient orange and brown couch.

"Mammi's drawings?" he asked.

Juliana nodded again. She had discovered the brown, leather-bound book in Opa's basement over Christmas: a collection of pencil sketches drawn by Opa's mother, whom Juliana had learned to call Omama. Juliana had known that Mom's family had emigrated from Romania, and that her parents had spoken German, but that was it. It was just enough for a grade-school assignment on heritage. No one had said anything more about it to her over the years, and it had never occurred to her to ask. Half her friends had grandparents from outside the country, so she didn't find her family's situation different or even interesting. But finding this book and discovering that her great-grandmother had made the drawings when she was the same age as Juliana had changed all that. Even the first drawing—one of an old-fashioned and simple kitchen—had awoken Juliana's curiosity, and she now tried her best to learn what she could about Omama from Opa.

Opa reached for the book and she passed it to him.

"You see?" Opa said, pointing to the people standing behind the coffin. "Those are probably members of Mammi's family."

"Do you remember any of them?"

Opa stared at the drawing. "I left my glasses in my room."

"I can get them!" Before Opa could even protest, Juliana dashed out of the living room, down the basement, back up to her bedroom to get her phone to record, and landed back on the couch.

"*Wie der Blitz!*" Opa said. At Juliana's confused look he translated, "Like lightning. You're very fast!"

Juliana stealthily turned on her phone while Opa slid his glasses on. She didn't know if he would allow her to record. Although she felt guilty about doing it secretly, she didn't want to forget a word he said.

"So you said this is a drawing of a funeral?" she asked, to give her recording a frame of reference.

He studied the drawing closer, letting his finger float just above the page to each face as he stared at each one.

"Yes. This is how the women prepared the body, always dressing the person in his nicest clothes."

Juliana shuddered at the thought of handling a dead body, but out of fear of derailing Opa from his story, she said nothing.

"As sad as funerals were for Mammi, she liked how everyone would get together to help each other and be with each other when someone died. In fact..." He thought for a moment. "Yes, I believe she said that when someone died, everyone who had been fighting with one another stopped fighting, as though it were a blessing from God. Everyone could...oh, what's the word...*vertragen*..." He tapped himself on his forehead a few times. "Ah, yes. Tolerate. They could tolerate one another."

Juliana had mixed feelings about that: on the one hand, it sounded really nice, but on the other hand, did people fight so much that Omama had to comment on that? Juliana returned her attention to the drawing.

"Do you know who the person is? The one who died?"

Opa lifted the book closer to his face, but after a few seconds, shook his head. "No. But I certainly recognize the people behind him." He pointed to a big man standing beside a smaller woman. "You can never forget this pair: a big man standing beside a small woman. This is Georg, Mammi's cousin. He was useless to his family."

Opa had said this last month about this man. After

doing a little online research herself, she had decided Georg must have suffered from post-traumatic stress disorder after fighting in World War I. Juliana had tried to explain this to Opa about this cousin, but he had refused to listen. Tonight, she was too exhausted to debate it again. Besides, so long as Opa was remembering, she would just listen.

"This is his wife, Eva." He pointed to the small woman. "A very kind woman but very sad. I don't believe she ever remarried. Ah!" He pointed to the next row of people. "These are Mammi's siblings: Luki-Bátschi, Anna-Néni, and Rosi-Néni. 'Néni' for 'aunt,' and 'bátschi' for 'uncle.' Look how young they look. Mammi really knew how to draw a person's face, don't you think?"

Luki, Anna, and Rosi. "Those are nice names. Did you know them?"

"You're sad because of Rachel, aren't you?" he said, abruptly changing the conversation.

"Uh, yeah," Juliana replied, surprised and disappointed. "But did you know Omama's siblings?"

"Katy tells me the two of you are very close."

Juliana's shoulders dropped. Opa's memory had apparently shut down again. She paused the recorder. "Rachel helped me a lot when I broke my wrist a few years ago, and I helped her when her parents divorced. It all happened pretty close together, and that's how we became really good friends."

"And you're sad not just because your best friend's mom

died, but because you can't be there." Opa placed his arm around her and pulled her in. "When someone dies, it's important to do your best to be there for them. But remember, too, Yulika, that others are also helping."

Juliana pulled away from Opa.

"I upset you?" he asked.

She didn't want to yell at him, but she was finding it hard not to.

"Omama spoke out too often," he said. "I think sometimes you don't speak out enough."

"I yell at my parents."

"Only because you don't speak to them about what is troubling you when it begins to trouble you. You wait too long to talk to them."

Juliana wanted to object and share with him how often she had calmly told them about not wanting to move, but she didn't want to insult Opa.

"Tell me what upset you," he asked again.

His elderly voice sounded so calming that she gave in. "I hate that she has others to look after her. I'm her best friend. I'm supposed to help her. That's what best friends do." She sniffled and blinked away her tears. "Mom said in the car on the way home that we can't afford to fly back, so I have to sit here while she deals with something so devastating. I can't do anything to help her." Juliana's sadness broke through and she cried. "I told Mom I could go by myself, and Mom said I'm not old enough and besides, I have dance and school and everything. So I'm stuck here and I feel like I can't do anything."

Opa offered her a tissue and gently rubbed her back.

Why was the whole world against her? Why couldn't she have a normal life, stay with the friends she'd grown up with, and hang out with Rachel? Why did Rachel's mom have to die now? Why did she have to die at all?

"I'm sorry," she eventually said to Opa. She blew her nose a few times. "It's just not fair."

Opa set the book on the table. "Yulika, you can only do what you can do. When someone dies, you need people who care about you to help you. Family and friends help out and work together. That's why this man's family is standing around him. They helped each other when he died. You have to help Rachel's family now."

"How can I do that from here?"

"Call her father. Or talk to her other friends. You have a computer. Can't it help you do that?"

Juliana hadn't thought of that; she had been too focused on Rachel. *And she probably has a ton of people trying to contact her.*

Opa stood up. "I have to go and watch the news now. Have a good night, Yulika." She listened as he shuffled his way into the kitchen, down the stairs and into the basement.

Juliana stared at the drawing of the coffin and the

people standing behind this man. Were any of them his best friend?

She picked up her phone. Although she didn't have Rachel's dad's phone number, she could message a few of her friends from her old studio. She logged in to her social media account and began.

CHAPTER SIX

"It's almost Easter," Mammi said to her children as they stood in the narthex of the church. "You've sat with the adults too often."

Although unconfirmed children in the church usually sat in the balcony, next to the organ, since Tata's departure, Elisabeth's siblings had occasionally gotten away with sitting with the adults. Mammi had allowed it during the Christmas season, and now every Sunday at least one of them begged to do it again. This new habit had tried Mammi's waning patience and her threats had become increasingly severe.

"For one hour in my life," she said to the children, "I'd like to concentrate on someone else besides you." Elisabeth could sympathize.

Today, Rosina was the one to dig in her heels but Mammi immediately pulled her by the ear, causing her youngest daughter to cry out in pain. To Elisabeth's dismay, several women nodded in approval as they passed by on their way to their pews.

"If you defy me one more time, you will kneel in the box of corn. People are talking about us and I will not have that any longer."

It had been several days since Mammi had begun resting as the midwife had instructed. To Elisabeth's joy, her mother's appetite had returned. But to her dread, Mammi had once again begun paying attention to the children's behaviour.

Rosina's lower lip turned down and began to quiver.

"I'll take them, Mammi," Elisabeth said, grabbing Rosina's hand. "We'll sit together," she said cheerfully.

"But I want Mammi," Rosina said with a pout.

"Shh...you'll be able to see her from upstairs. Luki, Anna, come along." Elisabeth led them up the stairs. When they reached the top, Elisabeth pointed out Mammi, who had sat down next to one of her sisters on the right side of the congregation. "See? There she is."

The women sat on the right, the men on the left, the elders at the front, and the children upstairs. This was except for the children who were confirmed but unmarried —the *großbuben* and *großmädchen*, as these older boys and girls were called. They sat to the side of the chancel, the slightly elevated stage beneath the pulpit. A year older than Elisabeth, Maria was already sitting there. She gave a little wave, which Elisabeth returned. Soon Elisabeth would be able to sit there, too.

"I'm not sitting next to Luki," Anna declared without reason and sat down on Elisabeth's other side.

Elisabeth sighed. Her confirmation couldn't come soon enough.

PASTOR FRÖHLICH STOOD IN THE PULPIT, A SMALL, RAISED speaking area above the altar and its painting of Jesus on the Mount of Olives. He had just finished reading the Gospel of Luke, chapter eleven, verses fourteen to twenty-three, where Jesus cast out the Devil from a blind, deaf, and mute man. Once the demon was gone, the man's afflictions disappeared. However, because not all men believed that Jesus had the power to cast out the Devil, they thought He might be the Devil himself.

"But we know how wrong they were," Pastor Fröhlich said from above the congregation. "For Jesus explains that He could not have cast out the Devil. If Jesus were indeed the Devil, and He cast out a demon, then the Devil's kingdom would be fighting within itself, thereby dividing itself. Jesus says in this Gospel, 'Every kingdom divided against itself is brought to desolation; and a house divided against a house falleth.' He means, then, that only because God is Jesus could Jesus cast out the demon. In other words, if we do not work with one another as a congregation, as one large family, we will become divided. And if each individual family in this congregation fights within itself, so, too, will they weaken and fall. I urge you during this time of Lent to look within and see if you are, as Jesus says, divided among yourselves. For if you are, your family will certainly fall, and so, too, will this church."

He paused to let everyone think about what he had just said. Elisabeth thought about her family's dislike for Tata's family and everyone's dislike for Mammi's mother.

Then it struck Elisabeth, like a bolt of thunder from heaven: disobeying her parents meant she was fighting them. Maybe that was why God commanded that all children honour and obey their parents: to keep the family together. Then all would be well and all would live a long life, as God said in His commandment.

But Mammi was wrong and the midwife was right, she recalled. *Am I causing my family to fall because I'm speaking up to help them?*

She felt like Jesus in the painting beneath the pastor, over the altar: He was kneeling, His hands open, His gaze directed up toward heaven, looking for answers.

EVERYONE NOW STOOD OUTSIDE, CROWDED AROUND THE little yellow church and beyond, spilling onto the street. The warm spring sun shone down, inviting all God's people to stay outside just a little longer before they returned home for lunch and an afternoon of visiting.

And Maria! Elisabeth thought, eagerly remembering her best friend's promise.

Luki had already disappeared to play with some friends from school, while Rosina had found the Bartolf family who lived on the corner by the Schuhmacher house and had gone to play with their daughters. Now one of Anna's friends waved at her and Anna happily waved back.

"Anna, no smiling. There's no need to look stupid," Mammi said and swatted her on the back of the head.

For some reason Elisabeth still could not understand, Mammi insisted that smiling reflected a lack of intelligence. Anna listened to her mother and stopped smiling, for which Elisabeth was grateful. Her sister could be a pitchfork in everyone's side if she wanted to be. Especially in Elisabeth's.

However, Elisabeth was thankful that Mammi was feeling better. Under the late morning sun, she almost seemed to glow. The change was remarkable, and Elisabeth promised herself that she would say an extra Lord's Prayer tonight as a thank you, before bed.

"You look much better, Mammi."

"Mhm," Mammi replied as she looked for her own circle of friends. That was enough for Elisabeth; she knew Mammi would not openly admit she was wrong. She did that about as often as Konrad-Bátschi and Margarethe-Néni said something nice.

Elisabeth scanned the crowd for Maria, hoping to tease more information out of her. Instead, though, Konrad-Bátschi and Margarethe-Néni walked over to her and Mammi. Elisabeth tried not to show her displeasure, but she always found them challenging. When their youngest daughter, Susi, had married last month, Konrad-Bátschi had demanded that each delicate *kipfel* be shaped into a perfect crescent, despite the fact that he had never baked in his life. Further, neither Elisabeth's aunt nor uncle had mentioned that Tata had written that first letter. If Elisabeth believed that Tata and Konrad-Bátschi had a tight bond between them, she would understand. But they didn't so Elisabeth believed that general kindness—something her aunt and uncle seemed incapable of—should have prevailed and they should have said something. There was also Konrad-Bátschi's belief that he was the better brother because he was the older one, Margarethe-Néni's 'compliments' that hid insults, and their treatment of Georg...the list in Elisabeth's head was long enough to fill Luther's *Small Catechism*.

Elisabeth's shoulders tensed, and she swore she even

heard a quiet grunt from Mammi. Remembering Pastor Fröhlich's sermon, Elisabeth made her usual request to Jesus for patience, fearing her anger could create a stronger divide in the family.

"Lissa," Margarethe-Néni said to Mammi, an unfriendly smile on her face. "How have you been? We haven't seen you in a few weeks except for church."

Mammi returned an identical smile. "Margarethe," she said in the same condescending tone, "I've been fine, thank you."

Margarethe-Néni leaned in a little. "Any news in the family?" She glanced at Mammi's waist. Elisabeth held her breath. Did she know? With Mammi's lost weight and numerous underskirts under her black overskirt, how could anyone tell she had a baby inside? Elisabeth wanted to slap her aunt: if Mammi didn't want to share anything about her condition, Margarethe-Néni should respect that. But one look at the bright yellow church and she knew she had to change her thoughts.

"We haven't heard more from my husband," Mammi said, "but that's understandable: the mail of course takes longer to travel over the ocean. But in his last letter he wrote that he's busy working in a factory and, when he has time, making shoes. He's earning very well."

Margarethe-Néni lifted her chin and pulled down on her *tschurak*, the light, black, fitted jacket that extended just past her hips, covering the waistline of her overskirt. "Konrad just received a large order from the Krehlings to repair some components for their mill. It will keep him and Georg very busy for a while," she bragged.

"If your son can hold himself together," Mammi said.

At that comment, Elisabeth bristled. Georg, along with Samuel and Stefan, had been very helpful these past few weeks, including taking Elisabeth out to the family's fields on Friday. There he had seemed uncharacteristically relaxed. He had even held a five-minute conversation with Elisabeth about planting, although Elisabeth had done most of the talking.

"You mean if you stop asking my son to help your family, the family my brother left behind," Konrad-Bátschi replied.

Mammi stood up straight. "My husband cares for his family," she declared. "Which is why he left. As for your son, Konrad, you can believe me: if there's one person I don't want helping my family, it's Georg." She flashed an angry look at Elisabeth. "My daughter still has a few things to learn." It was a phrase Elisabeth had heard before and meant Mammi would try to change Elisabeth's mind about something.

Mammi straightened her navy apron and tightened the knot of her black headscarf under her chin. "Well, we must find my other children. It's good to know, though, that we can agree on one thing, isn't it?" She grabbed Elisabeth by the wrist. "It's time for lunch."

Before Elisabeth could say anything or even think another thought, Mammi dragged her as she marched off toward Anna who, along with two other girls, was chasing a group of boys through a grove of trees.

CHAPTER SEVEN

'm so sorry!

Hugs!

OMG Rachel how sad.

#why

I'm so sorry!

Aunt Anne and all six of her kids were crowded in the kitchen visiting with Opa for a few minutes after school, an occasional tradition of sorts that had begun a few years ago, or so Juliana had heard. But Juliana had no desire to say hi to them. Instead, she was scrolling through her social media feeds and reading all the comments that everyone was leaving for Rachel, who had finally announced that her mom had died.

Juliana had received a few replies to the messages she'd sent last night as Opa had suggested, but all she got was a handful of empty thumbs-up emojis or bland responses like, "Oh, that's so sweet of you, Juliana. I'll let you know!" But no one had even bothered to tell her when the funeral was: Juliana had found out on social media. The funeral details were posted while she was in class, so dozens had already commented on the announcement.

OMG Rachel your #mom was such a wonderful woman! #momsrule

We're so sorry for your loss.

I hope that driver rots in hell! What an @%!#!

How are you feeling?

The question hung in front of Juliana's eyes. She wanted to know, too, but Rachel hadn't responded to any of these messages either. She read on:

I'll give you big hugs when I see you.

I'll see you tomorrow Rach. Call me if you need anything.

"Rach?" Juliana yelled. She threw her phone into her pillow. "That's what I call her and that's supposed to be my job!" Instead of Juliana being there for Rachel, it was other friends from Rachel's school and from their old dance studio. Of course Juliana loved them all—she could never forget how everyone had rallied around her when she had injured herself on stage and couldn't dance for months.

But she and Rachel had had special sleepovers, pulled all-nighters in the summer, watched their favourite movies together, and eaten chocolate until they felt sick. When her parents divorced, Rachel had stayed over at Juliana's a few times just to get out of the house.

How could all of that go into one post of support? "Call me if you need me" sounded cold, especially because someone else had already said it. Besides, Juliana had said exactly that to Rachel on the phone the first night they talked, before Kim had died.

If Juliana wrote what she was really feeling—that her insides were tearing apart and she didn't know from one minute to the next whether she'd break down and cry— she'd be breaking her promise to herself.

Juliana's texts to her old friends offering help had barely been answered. Was it because everything was looked after? Or because everyone was angry at Juliana for leaving?

If Juliana posted, would she look jealous, especially because she was so late in the long list of condolences? But if she didn't post, she'd look like an uncaring friend.

She had been one of the gang, and now she felt like that awkward new dancer, the one everyone's nice to and feels badly for but no one wants to befriend. *Wouldn't be the first time, I guess*, she thought, thinking back to how she'd felt when she'd first started at Kitchener Dance Academy just after Christmas. At the same time, many of those posting online right now were her old friends. *I shouldn't be feeling this way*, Juliana thought. She kept reading.

We're so sorry for your loss.

Our condolences, Rachel.

So sorry to hear that.

Half the posts were people apologizing. For what? How useful was it to apologize when you couldn't do anything to change what had happened?

Someone knocked on Juliana's door. "Can I come in?"

It was her cousin Sophie, who, at twelve, was the closest girl cousin in age to Juliana.

"Yeah, sure," Juliana said.

Sophie opened the door and cautiously stepped inside. "Hi," she said. Her blonde hair was tied into a ponytail. "I heard you yell a minute ago. Are you okay?"

The two stared at each other, although Juliana didn't know just how much of her Sophie saw: several years ago Sophie had been diagnosed with a disease that slowly made her go blind from the centre of her field of vision outwards. That was how Mom and Aunt Anne had explained it. So she could sort of still see, but not everything.

"Maybe that was a dumb question," Sophie said, still standing in the doorway. "I'm sorry about your friend's mom."

"Thanks," Juliana replied, though she didn't know why she felt compelled to say that, especially to another apology.

"How are you feeling?"

Juliana shrugged and then remembered her cousin's

lack of sight: she needed to keep reminding herself of it, especially because Sophie always looked directly at Juliana. "Don't know. Sad, I guess. Everyone's pouring out their heart to Rachel online, and I don't know if I should say something or not."

Sophie tilted her head to one side. "Why shouldn't you say something?"

Juliana didn't feel like explaining herself right now, but she didn't want to be rude either. "I don't know. I just don't know what others will think. I can't see them. Do they think I've left her behind now that I live here? Will they think I don't care if I post now at, like, spot number fifty? Or are all of these comments meaningless to her and I look stupid to her because she thinks I should know better?"

Sophie finally closed the door behind her and sat down in Juliana's office chair.

"I sort of know how you're feeling," Sophie said.

"You've lost someone?"

Sophie shook her head. "I mean with my eyes. If you have tears in yours right now, for example, I can't see them. It's like I can't see what you're thinking. If that makes sense."

Juliana felt embarrassed about her comment now. She hadn't thought about that. She stammered as she tried to apologize.

"Please, don't," Sophie said. "I really just meant it as I said it. I know what it's like when you can't see what you really want to see. If there's one thing that annoys me more than anything else with this stupid disease, it's that people start reading into everything I say."

Juliana didn't know how to respond. She could see how frustrating that would be for Sophie, and she certainly didn't want to add to it. Should she apologize? Or would that make things worse? "I hate this!"

"What?"

"Not knowing what to say! I don't want to hurt your feelings, but I don't want to make you feel worse. And I don't know what to put in this stupid Instagram post, if I say anything at all. I hate this!"

Both girls fell silent. Had Juliana just insulted Sophie? If Rachel had been sitting opposite her, Juliana would've known right away: Rachel would have combed her fingers through her hair while staring at the ground. But here in Kitchener, in this gray city with empty light rail tracks and tiny hills that looked like a kid's rollercoaster compared to the jagged, towering Rockies, Juliana knew no one. Her family until now had been—at most—small faces on a computer screen. The only familiarity for her was her dancing, but Kim's death had drained Juliana of any desire to even tap her toe right now.

"I think if I was your friend," Sophie said, "I'd be happy to see your name. As for me, it doesn't matter. I actually rarely tell anyone what I just said. I just felt comfortable telling you. I trust you, somehow."

"Somehow?" Juliana had to smile at that. "I guess I'll take that."

Sophie smiled, too.

Juliana said, "Okay, then. I will post something."

Sophie stood up. "I know I'd like to see my best friend's name there if something that sad happened to me." She reached for the door, but Juliana didn't want her to leave.

"Sophie, do you want to stay? I just need a minute to type this out. But I could use someone to just, I don't know, chat with."

A smile spread across Sophie's face and she plopped back down in Juliana's office chair, accidentally tipping it backwards and startling herself. Sophie's cheeks turned red, and then both girls burst out laughing.

"I'll be home in time to take you to dance," Mom said on the phone. "I'm really sorry—three people called in sick today, including the assistant manager, and I can't get anyone else in until six."

"Whatever," Juliana said. She was barely listening and instead was staring at the still-growing list of condolences on her social media feeds.

"Juliana, if I could be there, I would."

"Yeah."

"I mean it."

"Sure."

"You can talk to Opa. I'm sure he'd be happy to talk to you."

"Sure."

"Jul—I'm sorry, honey, I have to go."

"Okay."

"I love you. You know that, right?"

"Bye."

There was a pause. "Bye, sweetie."

Juliana hung up the phone and started crying again. Kim's funeral had taken place just two hours before, and she hadn't been there. The last thing Juliana wanted to do was ask Rachel to stream it for her. That just felt wrong on too many levels.

Your mom would be proud of you. #why

I know she was watching from above.

You looked so beautiful.

You're so strong to deal with this.

I'm not strong, Juliana thought. She hadn't spoken with Rachel in two days. She'd tried texting her yesterday, but all she got was a really fast "can't right now" response, and that was it. Nothing today. *She's probably too busy*, she thought.

Suddenly her phone rang. Her heart rate sped up as she grabbed it, only to see Aunt Anne's number. "Really? Now?" She let the call go to voicemail. She would only answer if it was Rachel. A few seconds later, the house phone rang. Juliana tried to ignore the shrill clang of the old ringer, but it pierced her ears.

"Hello?" she heard Opa say through the paper-thin walls. A few seconds later, she heard his slow, heavy footsteps come down the hall. He opened the door, a gentle smile on his face, and handed her the phone. The whole phone, since he didn't have a cordless one in the house.

Juliana thanked him. "Hello?" she said, watching Opa leave, his head down as he carefully stepped over the cord.

"Hi, Juliana. It's Aunt Anne. How are you feeling?"

"Oh, hi. Um, okay, I guess."

"Your mom said today was really hard for you."

Juliana rolled her eyes. Did Mom have to tell everyone everything? "Yeah."

"Listen—I know you love dance, but I thought tonight you might just want to take a break from everything but maybe still not be alone." Aunt Anne paused, as though she was expecting a response.

"Um, maybe, I dunno."

"Why don't you just come over here and hang out with Sophie? I know you've got a competition coming up—I remember those days, for sure—but something tells me you're going to have a hard time concentrating anyways. I think your teacher would understand."

"You danced?"

"Sure. Your mom and I are only two years apart, so Tata

and Modr put us both in. Only, I had quit by the time I was twelve, I think. Or was it eleven?"

Now that Aunt Anne had mentioned it, it did sound familiar to Juliana, like a distant memory.

"I see."

"So? Do you want to come over?"

As much as Juliana loved dance, she had to admit that her aunt was right. Monday night had been bad enough, and Juliana knew she wouldn't be any better tonight.

"Okay," she said.

"Great. I'll let your parents know."

"What about Opa?"

"He's got his cereal. He'll be fine, Juliana. For once, you don't have to worry about someone else. Call your studio, let them know, and then come over. I'll expect you here in about twenty minutes."

After Juliana hung up, a wave of relief washed over her. No crowded dance studio tonight, and just time with family. Even if she hardly knew her family, they certainly knew her well. Maybe that was all she really needed tonight: a few people who knew what would be good for her, because she didn't know what she needed herself.

AUNT ANNE AND UNCLE PHILLIP'S HOUSE WAS OLD, LIKE THE rest in the neighbourhood, but had an extensive addition on the back. Each of the six kids had their own bedroom, the kitchen table sat ten, and the family room had enough couches and chairs for even more than that. The last time Juliana had been over was at Christmas, but there had been so many people here that it felt crowded. Now, with just Aunt Anne, Scott, Sophie, Dean, and Charlie—Uncle Phillip was still at work and the two oldest cousins were who knows where—Juliana could feel the space, and it almost felt like her old home in Calgary, though with a few extra bedrooms. She checked her phone in case Rachel had texted, but there was nothing.

"Come on in," Sophie said. "Mom made us some popcorn. I really wanted to watch one of the singing shows tonight. But if you wanted to watch something else..."

Juliana shook her head. "No, that sounds fun and mindless."

Aunt Anne was in the kitchen, finishing up with the popcorn. She came out to the living room, offering each girl a bowl. "Flax oil and salt. Katy told me that a few years ago, and to be honest, it tastes better than butter."

Juliana smiled. She had to agree. It was something Mom had read online ages ago, switching her family's popcorn topping and then broadcasting it to everyone she knew. Juliana happily accepted her portion, and she and Sophie sat down on the couch. Sophie reached for the remote, pressed a few buttons, and turned on the television. How could she see those buttons but not be able to read a book? There was so much to Sophie's eye disease Juliana couldn't figure out.

A contestant walked onto the stage looking supremely confident. His hair was coiffed, long bangs hanging just into his eyes.

"Ugh," Juliana said. "Why do guys think that's cool?"

"What is?"

Juliana described the guy's hairstyle. "And then—yup, there it is—they flick their head to the side to get their bangs out of the way. If they'd just cut them, they could save themselves the effort."

Sophie burst out laughing. "Now that makes sense. There's this guy in my class, and I could never figure out why his head kept twitching to the side. I mean, I could see his hair move, but I didn't know it was hanging in his eyes!"

Juliana joined in. "It's like how they get women to do that on all those hair commercials—"

"And your neck just hurts watching them swing their hair all over the place!"

"Yeah!"

Both girls kept laughing but stopped the moment the contestant began his song. He launched into a rendition of "Amazing Grace," and both girls' jaws dropped.

"Wow..." Sophie said, and it was the only word uttered. The clarity and range of his voice astonished them. The female judge broke into tears, and it didn't take long for Juliana to do the same. She sniffled.

"Are you okay?" Sophie asked. "Do you want to watch something else? I can change—"

"No, it's okay, really," Juliana replied.

"We've got tissues somewhere."

Juliana saw the box on a side table and grabbed it. "I don't know a lot of church or gospel music, but it reminded me of today. It was the funeral."

"Oh."

An uncomfortable silence filled the air and the girls listened to the judges give their feedback.

"But your hair," the female judge said. "You need to stop flicking it. It's distracting."

Both girls broke into a fit of giggles and Juliana had to quickly grab a tissue before her nose exploded.

CHAPTER EIGHT

Elisabeth handed Anna the last plate. Anna dried it and passed it to Rosina who put it away. Luki was sitting in the front room trying to build a house with Tata's playing cards. Mammi took another cloth and wiped down the wooden kitchen table.

"Mammi, we can finish up," Elisabeth said.

Elisabeth hadn't seen Mammi clean so fast in a while: her hands blurred as they alternated moving in big circles to dry the table. "I'm almost done," she snapped. Without looking up, she then said, "You are not to have anything to do with that family. Not with their crazy son, their lame son, their stuck-up daughters...no one."

"But—"

Mammi slapped the table and glared at Elisabeth. "No one! We will get through your father's absence on our own if we must. I do not wish to be indebted to those monkeys because you've accepted their son's help."

"But how—"

"Enough!" Mammi said. She pointed a finger at Elisabeth. "You have begun an evil habit of disobeying me. You are not too old to kneel in that box of corn kernels. Have I made myself clear?"

Elisabeth nodded.

Mammi dried the table and Elisabeth and her sisters worked silently alongside her to finish up. Once they were done, Elisabeth insisted everyone go into the front room while she took the slop pail out to the pigs. Even just a few minutes of quiet would help her regain a little peace.

Just as she was about to slip on her boots, though, she saw a familiar face coming up along the side of the house. She opened the door and welcomed Maria in. They kissed each other on both cheeks. Maria lifted a leather satchel over her head and placed it on the floor.

"Don't touch!" she said playfully.

Her smile changed Elisabeth's mood immediately. "It's been torture waiting these last few days!" she said. She invited Maria in and explained she had one more chore to finish. Maria passed on greetings to the Schuhmachers from her family while Elisabeth took out the slop pail.

Once Elisabeth returned, Maria giggled in a way that showed she was pleased with herself for this little trick.

"You're going to love this!" she exclaimed. "But we need

to sit somewhere first. This is very special and can't get dirty."

Elisabeth led Maria to the back room. Although the kitchen would have been suitable and certainly warmer, the farther away Elisabeth was from Mammi right now, the better she could relax and enjoy her friend's visit. Elisabeth couldn't reconcile Mammi's demand that she not have anything to do with Tata's family with the fact that his nephews had been a great help to her.

But for now, Elisabeth had a happy diversion to take her mind off all that.

The girls sat on wooden chairs and Maria slowly opened the satchel, watching Elisabeth with a playful grin as she did so. Elisabeth couldn't sit still and kept bouncing in her chair. Maria pulled out the magazine from America and lay it on the table.

The front cover was mostly red. The words at the very top were in a language Elisabeth couldn't read. Underneath it were drawn the bottom half of a woman wearing a skirt that hung a few centimetres above her ankles, a white dog with black spots on a leash the woman was holding, and then the backs of two men. One appeared to be dressed casually, wearing a peach jacket and gray hat, and the other formally, in black and white.

"Look," Maria said as she opened the magazine and began leafing through the pages. "The women dress so elegantly and modern!"

Elisabeth's eyes were wide as Maria paged through the magazine. Fur coats, short hair, even lipstick.

"Are they all unmarried?" Elisabeth asked.

Maria giggled kindly. "You are sometimes so naive, Lissika," she said, continuing to turn pages. "Modern women don't cover their hair once they're married."

"Wait, stop there," Elisabeth said, and Maria held the magazine open to the image of a particularly striking woman in a sleeveless gown that hung past her feet. A long piece of fabric—a large shawl, perhaps?—lay draped over her left arm, leaving only her hand visible. Elisabeth couldn't tell what the woman's hair looked like, but it was held in place by a laurel wreath.

"Do all American women dress like this?" Elisabeth asked.

"I don't think so. Look at these ones." She flipped through farther in the magazine and opened up to a page of women each holding a stick with a bulb at the end over their shoulders, looking like they were about to swing it. One wore a skirt but the other two wore...pants? The woman in the middle had on baggy pants that stopped mid-calf.

"That looks just ugly!" Elisabeth exclaimed. "All of them. Those pants are horrendous! They make the women look like men!"

Maria giggled. "Don't they?" She feigned a shiver at the thought.

"I'm sure these women don't have husbands."

Elisabeth now turned the pages, giggling at some images but staring in awe at others, especially the women in their fashionable dresses.

"I think this is what some of the rich women in Arad must wear," Elisabeth said.

Thirty-eight kilometres away, Arad was the centre of Arad County, to which Semlak belonged. But to reach it required a trip by horse over the Marosch River—either by cable ferry or over thick ice—to a nearby train station, and then a train ride. Elisabeth hoped to go there someday herself, but she knew that would be out of the question for a while. Besides not having enough money for the trip, Elisabeth and her family simply had too much work to do with Tata away.

Maria nodded in agreement. "Actually, Mammi and Tata said that if the river ice melts before planting time and the cable ferry is running again, then they might take me to Arad for several days."

Elisabeth clapped her hands. "How exciting! Tata bought my book there last summer. I'd love to see the store where he bought it."

What she didn't say was that she felt jealous. Maria's mother, Haibach Anni, had come with a large dowry—her parents, the Krehlings, owned a good deal of land and the flour mill Konrad-Bátschi would be doing some work for—

and Maria's father, Haibach Adam, was one of the best wain-wrights in the village. Even farmers and business people who weren't German Lutherans sometimes came to him to help with their wagons. The Haibach family also kept a number of pigs they sold at market and exported to Germany.

By contrast, the Schuhmachers didn't have enough money to buy any extra land that would help Tata grow extra feed to keep extra pigs, or even to harvest extra wheat to sell at the market. The Schuhmachers were self-suffi-cient: neither rich nor poor.

"That's not all I have to show you," Maria said. She pulled a postcard out of her satchel.

"What is that?" Elisabeth took the postcard. The picture was of a rather large, plain house with two floors of small windows.

"A cigar factory from Harrisburg."

Elisabeth gasped. "Is this where Tata works?"

"Turn it over."

Elisabeth jumped out of her chair. Tata had written!

To my dear family,

I trust you received my first letter. I have not received your reply yet. But when I saw this postcard, and knew Maria would be sent a gift, I had to ask if I could include this. The factory I work in looks like this one. I am earning well and am saving all I can. I hope you are all doing well. I also know my Golden One will be confirmed soon. Study hard, like I know you can, Elisa-

beth. Jesus is watching. And please give my regards to my brother.

Love,

Your Tata

Golden One was what Tata called Elisabeth sometimes. She bent over and wrapped her arms around Maria, who was still sitting. "I can't wait to show Mammi and my brother and sisters!" She took one step toward the door and stopped.

"What?" Maria asked. "Is something wrong?"

Elisabeth sat back down. "Mammi got into a fight outside church today with Tata's family. This afternoon, Mammi forbade me from having anything to do with them again, and now Tata asks in his postcard to give his regards to them. I don't want to get Mammi upset again." *Especially with her baby*, she thought, though she couldn't say that.

An uncomfortable silence followed. Maria intertwined her fingers and stared at her hands. She looked like she wanted to say something but was too scared to.

"What is it?" Elisabeth asked.

Maria still stared at her hands.

"Best friends tell each other the truth."

Maria smoothed out her apron, but she still would not look up. "People are saying that you should not be spending time with Georg if you know what's good for you."

Elisabeth could hardly believe her ears. She and her

cousin were the topic of the rumour mill? "What's good for me? What's that supposed to mean?"

Maria cautiously looked up, scratched her nose and ran her hand over her braided hair. Was it that serious that Elisabeth's best friend couldn't answer her question directly?

"It means...you'll have a hard time finding a good husband if Georg is one of your friends."

Elisabeth banged her fist on the table. "He's a member of my family! What do they expect me to do: get rid of him?"

Maria jumped in her chair at Elisabeth's outburst. Elisabeth tucked a few wisps of hair behind her ears and lowered her chin. "I'm sorry," she said in a quieter voice. "I just don't see why this is anyone's business."

"They're afraid Georg will kill anyone he doesn't like. No one would want to marry someone...associated...with him."

"Why...? How...?" Dozens of questions formed in Elisabeth's mind, but they all jumbled into one mess that couldn't untangle itself, leaving her speechless.

Maria adjusted her apron again. "When he gets all crazy, he sometimes pretends to shoot people. People are saying he's imagining who he'll kill next."

"People? What people?" Elisabeth wanted names.

"Wagner Anna said she heard it from Tiny Hay, who's of course cousins with Stefan, who's Georg's only friend, so he may have said something, but Omi heard from Hagel Samuel who heard it from Meier Josef who actually saw it, but I think he also heard it from Müller Anna who also told—"

"All right," Elisabeth said. "In other words, everyone."

Maria leaned in, looking a little perplexed. "Haven't you seen him? He has at least one episode a week, though I hear lately it's been more."

Elisabeth sighed. She disliked gossip, but at the same time, what else was there to talk about? She explained the one time she had seen Georg collapse in a fit of shakes in his home and how she had seen her aunt slap him in a futile attempt to force him to stop. "But he didn't look like he was shooting anyone—he looked like he was seeing something horrible."

"Probably what will happen to him if he does kill someone." Elisabeth gave Maria a disapproving look. "Fine, fine, that was too harsh. But what else would he see? How many men went to war and came back fine? Look at your father."

Elisabeth had to admit that Maria was right. Tata had been to war, and although he never talked about it, he didn't shout out like his nephew or collapse—as Mammi had once described Georg—like a sack of potatoes.

"I feel sorry for your father," Maria continued. "To be related to someone like that, and who's the oldest son in his own family, no less. All your uncle's land will go to him instead of your fine family." She shook her head. "That must be embarrassing."

Elisabeth hadn't thought of it that way before. If Mammi didn't want her spending time with Tata's family, and Tata was embarrassed by Georg's behaviour, then maybe she should obey their wishes. Tata probably just wanted Elisabeth to pass on his greetings to be polite. But what could she do about the fact that Georg had helped her out several times precisely because Tata was away?

"No, Maria, that can't make sense. Tata and Konrad-Bátschi don't get along—everyone knows that—but Tata has always tried to at least be nice to him and his family, or if not nice, then at least polite. But Georg helped me on our fields on Friday, and with the pigs and all of that mess. Never once did he look like he was going to kill someone. Not even Hagel Samuel."

Maria's expression became serious. "Lissika, you see so much good in people, I think you sometimes aren't careful enough. Just because Georg is good for a few minutes once in a while doesn't mean he isn't crazy. I even heard some people say they might stop bringing their shoes to your family, especially because you forced Hagel Samuel to work with him."

Elisabeth jumped out of her chair. "What?! Because Hagel Samuel couldn't keep his son in line to properly fix our animal stalls?" She paced up and down the room. "What would they have me do? Fix the stalls myself? They have no idea what's happening here." She shot a look up at the crucifix. *Jesus, how can You let this happen?*

"What do you mean?" Maria asked.

Elisabeth realized she'd almost told Mammi's secret. "Just... just..." She tried to think of something to say. "Just that Tata's away, we have no other men in the house, Mammi's brothers aren't much help—Omama even spent a week here when that whole pig problem happened because Peter-Bátschi and Sophie-Néni couldn't keep their children under control—and the war has taken many good, strong men from us. I'm doing my best to help Mammi. What do people expect?"

Maria tucked the magazine back into her satchel. "They expect you to act like a woman, Lissika. To know where your place is, to let the men do their work, and to associate with the right people." She passed Elisabeth the postcard. "Your father only says to give his regards to his family, not to help them, be kind to them, or anything like that. He's being polite, as you said. No one is asking you to be rude, just to stop spending time with them. You know these rumours will pass, but only if you stop feeding them."

Elisabeth held the postcard in her hands. Both Tata and Mammi would want Elisabeth to act in the best interests of the family, and she did not want to be the one to cause the family to fall, as Pastor Fröhlich had warned. *Maybe that's why Tata tries to be nice to his brother: to keep his family together.* She suddenly felt an even deeper respect for her father and even more scorn for Konrad-Bátschi.

"I will try," she said.

"I'm sorry," Maria said. "I didn't want to hurt your feelings. But we both want to marry well, and we can only do that if we know what others think about us."

Maria changed into her boots at the house door while Elisabeth got her shawls.

"To be honest," Maria said, "I do feel sorry for Georg. Whatever is causing these shakes, it's embarrassing enough for him, and I think the others are being too cruel. But if these shakes are God's punishment, then is everyone's behaviour wrong? What if the people are helping God punish Georg?" She threw her satchel over her shoulder.

Elisabeth hadn't thought of that either. Luther preached that God punished those who did not follow His word, and she remembered Luther's admonishment about anyone who did not follow the Ten Commandments. Georg had been a frightening and scornful man before the war. Maybe God was finally paying attention. Maybe Georg's shakes were indeed of his own doing and he wasn't taking responsibility for them.

Mammi was right: Elisabeth should stay away from Tata's family.

She glanced at the postcard. *I'm sorry,* she thought, *but this time I need to disobey you and listen to Mammi.*

A few hours had passed since Maria's visit, and Elisabeth had shown her family the postcard immediately afterwards, despite the risk of angering Mammi, because Elisabeth knew she would want to see it. Mammi had allowed herself a tiny smile upon reading Tata's message, but she had forbidden Elisabeth from passing on his greetings to his family.

After everyone had seen the postcard—and her siblings had almost ripped it into pieces out of excitement—Elisabeth had tucked it away in a special box for safekeeping. Mammi had then lain down and Elisabeth had sent her siblings outside to play.

Luther's *Small Catechism* now lay on the dining table in the back room, open to the Lord's Prayer. It was Elisabeth's reward for having successfully memorized his interpretations of each of the Ten Commandments. She had skipped over the third petition—the one about doing God's will— had memorized the fourth one, and was now trying to memorize the fifth petition, *Forgive us our trespasses as we forgive those who trespass against us*. But despite her best efforts to focus, her conversation with Maria unendingly repeated itself in her mind. The rumours traveling through the congregation about Elisabeth angered her. She wanted to defend herself, but what if that angered people enough that they truly did not bring their shoes to Mammi anymore? Without produce or livestock to sell, Tata's shoe-making business was the Schuhmachers' only source of income in the winter.

"Why can a man go to war, kill people with his weapons, and when he returns, he's celebrated a hero?" she asked Jesus on the wall. "But when a girl stands up for her family, they speak ill of her?" It didn't seem fair. When would they forgive her for her trespasses?

Unable to answer her questions, she pushed the book aside and pulled out her book of drawings. She needed to get something out of her, and if speaking wasn't allowed, then she would use her pencil. Tata had given her the book so she could sketch the important events of the year while he was away, but she felt a different urge within her now, a new one, one propelled by something powerful that would only leave through her hand. She opened the book up to a fresh page and stared at it. What did this feeling want her to draw? All she felt right now was frustration at not being able to figure out what was right and wrong, and anger at the unfairness of it all. How could she draw frustration? Unfairness? Anger?

The lantern's flame flickered inside its glass container, enchanting her. "And if I raise the wick..." Elisabeth turned a knob on the lantern that raised the wick inside the glass. "...then the flame becomes too strong and begins to dance wildly, out of control. If I lower it—" and she did—"then the flame is under control." She raised and lowered the wick, the flame almost burning its image into her eyeballs.

This yearning inside her compelled her to draw the lantern, though she didn't understand why. She lowered the wick before the glass got too hot and began to outline the flame in her book. She sketched, shaded, and smudged her strokes, and as the lantern on the page took form, Elisabeth realized what she was drawing: her anger.

CHAPTER NINE

Juliana stayed in the car, even though she and Mom had reached the studio. It was Saturday morning practice.

"I still think I could've flown back home," she said. "We had time to find a last-minute flight." Although Juliana had had fun with Sophie the night before, returning to Opa's house reminded her of how unfair it was that she hadn't been able to stand alongside her best friend. Juliana had had a fitful sleep, and all she could think about was how easy it would've been to fly back to Calgary for the funeral.

"I know you're upset—" Mom began.

"You have no idea!"

Mom undid her seatbelt and turned to face her. "Juliana Elizabeth Roth—"

"Oooh, the middle name."

"That's enough. We're all sad for Rachel and Rhys."

"Not as much—"

"You didn't work with her for four years! Kim and I were pregnant together! I would have also liked to fly back, but it wasn't possible. We don't have twelve hundred dollars we can just drop like that!" Mom gripped the steering wheel, took in a deep breath and let it out, and then placed her hands back in her lap. "I'm sorry. It seems like this is getting to me, too. But we have to move on. Your dance team is waiting for you."

Juliana folded her arms over her chest. "I need to be with Rachel."

Mom sighed, signaling she was no longer angry. "I know you do. And I'm sorry your father and I couldn't make that happen."

Juliana ripped her bag out of the backseat, slammed the car door after she had gotten out, and didn't look back as she strode off to dance class.

THE DRUM BEAT IN THE MUSIC SEEMED LOUDER TO JULIANA than usual. Was it her? Or had Miss Denise turned the music up? Either way, it reverberated through her body with an intensity that mirrored her anger.

STAMP

It's not fair that I'm here and not back home!

TURN TURN TURN LEAP

And that Rachel has to do this without me!

STAMP SHUFFLE BALL-CHANGE STOMP CRAMP-ROLL TOE STAMP

And that I have to go through this without her!

FLAP FLAP FLAP FLAP FLAP FLAP FLAP FLAP

FLAP BALL-CHANGE FLAP BALL-CHANGE STAMP CRAMP-ROLL STOMP HIT

Her anger and the music whirled together inside her and then shot into her feet, out of her hands, straight through her heart, up her spine, and out of her head. Her arms thrust into each position as though she was trying to break through a brick wall. When she turned, every whip of her head happened so fast that she almost believed her eyes never left their focus at the front. It was as though she was spinning on a spindle, perfectly balanced, her energy wrapping itself around her and sling-shotting out of her.

HEEL FLAM HEEL STAMP HEEL FLAM HEEL STOMP

What's happening to me? she thought as the music, her anger, and her feet seemed to carry her through the choreography.

Miss Denise stopped the music to explain a few corrections. Juliana shook her hands, impatient to start again. Not dancing bottled up her energy and she needed to move to let it out. Miss Denise rewound the music, everyone took their previous positions, and she counted them in.

STAMP SHUFFLE BALL-CHANGE STOMP CRAMP-ROLL TOE STAMP

The energy once again shot out throughout Juliana's body like the heat of an immense fire that could no longer be contained.

This is all unfair! Of course Juliana couldn't ask Rachel to stream her mother's funeral, casket and all. And yet Juliana wanted to see everything, as though seeing it all would help her feel like she had been there. Without having seen the ceremony or interment, Juliana felt excluded and like she would never be able to share this life-changing event with Rachel. Ever.

Flap ball-change flap ball-change stamp cramp-roll stomp hit

But she and Rachel had already supported each other through tough times. Although Kim's death was a million times worse than an injury or divorce, Juliana and Rachel had already proven to one another that they would do whatever they could to help each other.

What if Juliana had actually done all she could do, even though it was practically nothing?

Hold five, six, seven, eight.

What was happening? With each movement, each step, each sound, the voice inside her head began to quiet.

Hit hit hit kick down riff...

By the time Miss Denise stopped the music this time, the angry shouting in Juliana's mind had transformed into a mere whisper.

With each pass of the group's tap routine, Juliana noticed that her feelings about other situations also eased: her anger about the move, her sadness about her parents' frequent absence, her disappointment about not being able to fly back to Calgary...all the pain and struggles of the past few months were moving out and through her body.

By the time class was over, Juliana couldn't cry if she wanted to, that energy replaced by an unexpected calm. She still felt sad and angry, but not...*explosive*, she thought.

As the class emptied out, the other dancers either stroked her arm or gave her hand a quick squeeze. The guys nodded in understanding. Juliana knew she was the weakest dancer in the class, but everyone accepted her: she wasn't that awkward new dancer anymore. That was something to be happy about, wasn't it?

"Juliana," Miss Denise said. "Can I speak with you for a moment?"

Juliana held her breath. Had she done something wrong?

"What you danced today..." Miss Denise paused and shook her head. "I've never seen you dance so well."

Juliana's eyes popped open.

"But don't think that makes you perfect," Miss Denise warned with a smile.

"I know!" Juliana jumped for joy and then ran out to join the others. Whatever was changing inside her, even if it started from something horrible, was turning into something...magical. How was that possible?

"Thanks for coming over," Juliana said to Jasmine as they sat at the kitchen table. "If there's one thing I have to face with all this, it's that just as much as Rachel needs people, I sort of do, too."

Jasmine nodded. "I get it. It's been a tough week for you."

Juliana turned her glass around on the table, mesmerized by the distorted tablecloth patterns through the water. "Rachel texted and said she'd be gone all weekend. Her dad said she couldn't take her phone."

"They probably have a lot to talk about."

"I guess so." Juliana took a sip of water.

Jasmine bit into a slice of orange. "Your life hasn't been easy these last couple of months, has it?"

Juliana shook her head.

"And you're home alone again, right?"

"Yup. Opa's at a meeting at the German club, something about a trip to Cuba in a few weeks. Mom's working until six today, and Dad's on his way back from Georgia."

"And you don't have any siblings."

"Nope. Just my mom's family. They're nice and all, but still..."

Jasmine shook her head. "You amaze me, Juliana. With everything you're going through and in such a short period of time." Jasmine's compliment surprised Juliana, because she believed there was nothing amazing about herself: she felt she was barely holding herself together. Furthermore, Jasmine was by far the better dancer. Juliana told her so.

"I plan to make it someday," Jasmine said. "And that takes practice and a lot of dedication." She took a sip of water. "But you today, I mean, what happened? You were so intense, like, on fire."

Juliana smiled at the compliment. "That's precisely how I felt. " She remembered Omama's drawing of a lantern. "Wait a minute...I want to show you something." She ran to her room and returned with Omama's book. "This book was my great-grandmother's drawing book. Like a journal. It has sort of helped me the last few weeks. I mean, not directly, but kind of...sort of...I don't know how to explain it."

Jasmine reached a finger out to touch the edge of the cover. Juliana had only ever seen Jasmine this attentive when their dance teachers spoke. She opened the book and found the picture of the lantern.

"This is exactly how I felt this morning in class. Like something in me was on fire, shooting heat all through my body, but it was still contained somehow, like it was traveling down pipes. Or something."

"I see what you mean. Look how much life that flame

has. That's exactly what you danced like. Something changed in you today, and I think what you're going through is a part of that. How incredible to have a picture from the past explain that to you." Jasmine gently turned a few more pages and then returned to the lantern. "My mom still remembers lanterns in her home village in Guatemala. She loved how they hung everywhere at night."

"Is that where your parents are from? When did they come here?"

"My mom. In the seventies. Has your grandfather told you about these pictures?"

"A few of them. Like how they didn't have a telephone back then, or what happened when someone died—that was actually kind of gross."

"I hope you didn't say that to him!"

Juliana laughed. "No, but I thought it, and now that we're talking about it again, I don't know if I'll be able to sleep tonight. Yuck. Women actually had to dress the body." She shuddered and both girls laughed. "But he's also telling me about my family some more. Neither of my parents ever talked much about their families. I don't know...it's kind of nice to know you don't come from nowhere."

"I hear you." She placed both hands on the table, signaling she was about to stand. "Listen, this is beautiful but you need a break from death. Why don't we head over to Belmont Village and get some ice cream?"

Juliana raised her eyebrows. "In the winter?" Even in Calgary, where it was regularly colder than Kitchener, Juliana wouldn't dream of eating ice cream at this time of year.

Jasmine smiled. "Or chocolate cake. Whatever you want. But we need to do something fun. You've had too much hard stuff lately."

Belmont Village was one of the best parts about living with Opa. It was a nearby street with shops and cafés. To get there, they had to cross a street and the Iron Horse Trail and then walk up a ramp to Belmont Avenue.

Both girls texted their parents. Mom and Dad sent Juliana a thumbs-up emoji almost immediately.

"Your parents okay with it?" Juliana asked.

Jasmine shrugged. "I just have to let them know where I am."

"That's cool."

"Sure." The tone in Jasmine's voice suggested she felt otherwise but judging by how Jasmine had changed the subject from talking about her parents, Juliana guessed she shouldn't ask more. "It's only minus twenty-one," Jasmine said, reading off her phone. "Should we make a run for it?"

"Only?" Juliana replied with a laugh. "I've done it in minus thirty!"

They put their boots on.

"Leave your bag here," Juliana offered. Both girls reached for their wallets when her phone buzzed again.

There's money in the money jar, Mom texted. *Treat yourselves.*

Juliana replied with an enthusiastic "Thank you" and pulled some bills from the money jar in the cupboard next to the fridge, stuffing them in her pocket.

She opened the side door and the two girls bolted out of the house and across the street, ignoring the sting of the frigid air in their lungs.

CHAPTER TEN

"A meeting of the administrative committee of Arad County will be held and the twenty-three communal secretaries will be appointed for each commune!" the postman announced. "There is a senate meeting to organize the rural constabulary!

"In the second half of February, two cases of diphtheria, one case of measles, one case of typhus, six cases of epidemic typhus, and one hundred and seven cases of Spanish flu have been reported to the sanitary services of the city of Arad!"

Elisabeth shook her head at the last piece of news. So many people sick with the Spanish flu. She shivered at the thought of it. Off in the distance, she saw children about Rosina's age playing with a ball. Was it the Spanish flu Luki and the three sisters had had? If so, she could only thank

Jesus for sparing their lives. But that this illness was still making people ill…?

"What do you think of this flu?" Elisabeth asked Georg and Stefan. Stefan had spotted her shortly after she'd arrived, and before she could find a way to disappear into the crowd, he and Georg had joined her to listen. *They came to me*, she thought, *and I'm only asking because I don't want to be rude.* But truth be told, Elisabeth wanted to discuss the topic with someone. The girls Elisabeth knew, including Maria, were only interested in gossip and any information that would help them secure a good husband. Only men discussed these topics, and two were standing next to her.

"Nothing," Georg said in his deep, quiet voice. He blew out smoke from his cigarette. Stefan began to open his mouth, but Georg touched him on the shoulder, and so he said nothing.

The mysteries of the world outside their village had affected Elisabeth's life too much for her to just ignore them. "Please tell me," she said. "I need to hear a thought that doesn't start with, 'But I want to knit!' Or 'You'll kneel in that corn if you don't listen to me!'"

Stefan chuckled at her imitations of her family and even Georg cracked a small smile.

"Please," Elisabeth pleaded. "I need to hear someone say something that doesn't involve anyone in this village."

Georg and Stefan exchanged looks, and finally Georg nodded to him.

"I would rather suffer and die of this flu," Stefan said, "than fight in that war and survive."

That response was not what Elisabeth was expecting. Didn't men eagerly anticipate going to war? She had been nine when war had been declared and she remembered hearing of the many parades that took place in the Banat, the large region that Semlak belonged to in the Austrian-Hungarian Empire. Everyone—men, women, and children—celebrated that they were defending their empire, avenging their assassinated crown prince, fighting for Hungary and Austria! Supporting Germany! When soldiers returned, sometimes during the war, and many at the end, there were tears, but Elisabeth always assumed they were tears of joy. She remembered feeling proud that Tata had served their country when he came home. She only realized now that no one had been celebrating combat or any kind of victory, regardless of the outcome of the war; they had been celebrating reunion. Repeating in her mind what Stefan had just said, Elisabeth shuddered: war was even more horrible than she had believed it to be.

"I'm sorry," she finally said. "Tata never spoke about it."

"Nor should he," Georg replied. "Your life continued here, normal for the most part. There's no need to give you the nightmares that many of us experience every day."

"Nightmares? But Tata never—"

"He repaired boots and shoes. He didn't fight. That made it easier for your father," Georg replied. Elisabeth hadn't known that.

Stefan pointed at the muddy ground. "Imagine living in this mud, Elisabeth, for days and weeks on end, sometimes even sleeping in it just to get some rest. Bullets and cannonballs fly over your head. You hear gunfire and explosions all day, some near you, some farther down the front."

Elisabeth tried to speak but her voice got caught in her throat and her eyes began to well up.

"You've said too much," Georg said.

"She wants to know, Georg. I can see the look in her eyes. I think more people should know what war was like, understand what we went through, what *you* went through."

"Heini! Throw to me!" a man called out from behind them. They turned as one of the boys laughed and threw the ball to the man.

Without warning, Georg's eyes got big and he dropped his cigarette. "Grenade!" he shouted and yanked both Elisabeth and Stefan down onto the muddy road. He had acted so swiftly that Elisabeth didn't know what had happened until her cheek hit the ground—she'd been able to turn her head in time. As the wet gravel pressed against her skin, she grew angry. What kind of rude joke was this? *Serves you right for not leaving right away,* she told herself.

A moment later, she heard laughter from those around them. Elisabeth pushed herself on to her knees, removed a mitten, and tried to wipe mud and gravel from her cheek. *This is just how Georg laughed at kids*, she thought. *Now they're laughing at him the same way.*

"Are you all right?" Stefan asked Georg. Georg didn't respond and Stefan called his name again. Georg began to shake and mumble. "He can't hear me," Stefan said to Elisabeth. "This isn't good."

It wasn't a joke. Georg had actually believed he was protecting them from death.

The boots of a man appeared in front of them. Elisabeth looked up and saw Peter-Bátschi, Mammi's sole brother, extending his hand. She took off her other mitten and offered him a clean hand, and he pulled her up. Elisabeth could smell alcohol on Peter-Bátschi's breath. This early in the day? It wasn't even lunchtime.

He whispered in her ear, "Leave him alone if you know what's good for you and my sister." The same words Maria had used.

"But—"

"Hold your tongue," he hissed. "Or do you want customers to stop coming to Lissa?"

Elisabeth clamped her mouth shut as her uncle took her by the hand and pulled her into the crowd without so much as acknowledging Georg and Stefan. Elisabeth wanted to leave the scene as fast as possible, but one more look at her cousin on the ground, and she knew he needed help, whatever the cause of his shakes and nightmares was.

"Scared of a children's ball, Georg?" Meier Josef shouted out.

"Is that what they threw at you on the front?" Hagel Samuel added. "Because they knew you couldn't handle the real thing?"

The crowd roared at the men's jokes. Elisabeth wanted to speak up, but Peter-Bátschi's hand gripped her tightly on the wrist, almost hurting her.

"Getting what you deserve, eh?" he shouted at Georg. "Is this your way of ruining my sister's family? By talking to her daughter, even though you're a married man!"

But he's my cousin! Elisabeth wanted to shout. This treatment of him was turning cruel.

Peter-Bátschi let go of Elisabeth's wrist and stepped again before the crowd. "Are you trying to ruin my sister's business?" he repeated. He looked ready to fight.

Elisabeth didn't know what to think. She believed Georg was in pain and that these fits were real, but she couldn't rid herself of the memories of the man Georg had been before the war, picking fights in the taverns— often winning because of his size—and pulling out the girls' braids, which he had often done to Elisabeth when she was Luki's age. He would even embarrass his mother in front of her friends and family, just like Konrad-Bátschi had his mother. Georg had been just like his father. *This must be his punishment,* she thought. *Maybe if Georg asked for forgiveness from everyone, these nightmares would stop.*

Stefan pushed himself on to his knees with his one arm. He wiped what mud he could off his face. The bits of clean skin that peeked through the mud were crimson. "Do you have any idea what we faced out there?"

"Sure!" Meier Josef shouted. "Running from balls!" Elisabeth now noticed Hagel Samuel, whose sister was Peter-Bátschi's wife, standing beside Meier Josef. He slapped him on the back in approval.

The crowd laughed at the joke while Georg continued to shake on the ground. He was doubled over, his hands in fists, as though he was fighting to prevent something from overcoming him. Stefan bent down again and continued calling his name.

"I fought and didn't run from children's toys!" Peter-Bátschi shouted. "Act like a man, Georg!"

"Maybe he's not a man," Hagel Samuel suggested to his brother-in-law. He sauntered up to Georg, who was still shaking, and planted his feet beside him. "Oh, look," he said, mocking a child's pout. "He's crying. Maybe he'd rather be a woman, so he can run and care for children and cook!" He spat on Georg, but Georg didn't react. Stefan had his good arm around Georg and couldn't push Hagel Samuel back. "And to think I had to help you." Hagel Samuel kicked Georg in the side, and Georg's body jerked in pain. Stefan glowered at Hagel Samuel, who only kicked more mud at him in response.

"Get up, you lazy mule!" Peter-Bátschi demanded, but Georg remained on the filthy ground.

Is he really crying? Elisabeth wondered in pity. The flame of anger inside her was ready to break through the glass: no matter how mean Georg had been, what he had really done or not in the war, or what he was trying to do now, he was a human being and a member of her family. He didn't deserve this. No man did. But worries about Mammi's shoemaking acted like a dark cloth over the lantern, dimming her resolve to act.

She heard shuffling in the crowd and turned around to see Pastor Fröhlich nudging his way through.

"What's going on here?" he asked as he stared at the scene before him.

Elisabeth watched as people in the crowd began to step back from Georg and exchange glances with one another.

"Nothing, Pastor," Meier Josef said.

"Just reminding Georg here of a few things," Peter-Bátschi added.

"Did no one hear my sermon on Sunday?" the pastor asked. "Where I spoke about being kind to one another to strengthen our congregation?"

Although many murmured some sort of agreement or briskly nodded, everyone scuttled on to their destinations, frequently glancing behind them. Peter-Bátschi hurried off, too, leaving Elisabeth by herself. She couldn't help but think the people who had laughed at Georg knew what they had done was wrong, because otherwise they wouldn't have been rushing to escape the pastor's questions. Those were not the actions of people carrying out God's orders: they were those of sinners.

She finally approached the two men. Stefan placed a hand on Georg's back and was whispering to him. Georg was still whimpering and shaking, but he managed to sit up.

"Georg," Stefan said finally. "It's over. You can go home now."

To Elisabeth's surprise, Georg's body relaxed and his chest expanded and contracted slowly again. Stefan rubbed his back a little, the way a friend does to comfort someone. The pastor offered him a hand, and Stefan pulled himself up.

"Can you stand by yourself?" the pastor asked Georg. "I'm afraid I'm not strong enough to help."

Georg's muscular body belied the weaknesses that plagued him on the inside. He nodded.

"Good," the pastor said. "People can be mean sometimes," he added. "Had I known what was happening, I would have come over sooner, but I thought it was just men discussing the week's headlines."

Georg stood up but his eyes remained focused on the ground.

"I must go," the pastor said. "I wish to see Herr Blum's school. Go home and rest. May Jesus be with you."

As the pastor began to walk away, Elisabeth blurted out, "Can you not help him?"

Pastor Fröhlich shook his head. "We are punished for our sins, Lissika, as Luther continually reminds us. This war has punished millions. Their healing is in Jesus's hands." He then looked at Georg who didn't seem to notice. "Pray for forgiveness. When you are forgiven, these fears will stop."

Elisabeth's heart sank. It was true: Georg was being punished. It may not have been through the congregation, as Maria had hinted, but these shakes and nightmares were his punishment.

Stefan spat on the ground, taking Elisabeth aback with his rude response to the pastor. "I have a hard time believing that millions deserved this," he said.

"Maybe we did," Georg said, his voice barely audible.

"How can you believe that?" Stefan asked. "I obeyed every word my parents said to the point where boys like you teased me to no end. In fact, you even punched me a few times when I walked home from school. I said 'please' and 'thank you,' stood up for my friends, helped my parents. I worked in the rain, the blazing sun...it didn't matter. I do not believe for a moment that I deserved this —" He gestured at his arm. "Or being imprisoned and kept from my friends and family for two years in Siberia. Do you really think that my arm will grow back once I've been forgiven?"

Georg shrugged and said nothing. "I'm sorry," he mumbled to Elisabeth. "I can have Eva wash—"

"No," she said. "It's all right. I can look after it." She wanted to part ways as quickly as possible, but she didn't know how to politely excuse herself.

It seemed no one knew what to do, because no one said or did anything. Elisabeth's emotions often got her in trouble for saying too much, but she had no words for this feeling. Yes, she was angry for the extra work this fit had caused her, and she was embarrassed at her own appearance, but one glance at Georg, and her anger was pushed aside by shame and pity for him. *But he's being punished*, she reminded herself. *This is not your concern.*

"Come," Stefan said to him, finally breaking the silence. "Let's get you home."

Words finally returned to Elisabeth and she said she needed to get something from the shop, even though she didn't. Mammi had demanded she not spend time with Tata's family, and Elisabeth knew that walking home with them—Georg's family lived close to hers—would confirm for any witnesses that she had chosen to spend time with them. *I don't need to kneel in corn on his account*, she thought.

"Thank you," Stefan whispered as he turned his friend around. Elisabeth nodded just enough to acknowledge that he'd spoken.

Aware of a draft in her ears, she reached to adjust her headscarf and only now realized it was hanging around her neck. She tied it back on her head. Trying to keep her chin high as she ignored pointing fingers and private whispers, she took a roundabout way home and promised herself that she would never spend time with Georg again.

But if this had indeed been his punishment, ordained by God as the pastor had said, then why did Elisabeth feel so uneasy about her promise?

Stefan's rebuttal to the pastor's words hung in her mind: would God punish millions? *Millions of men*, she added. The war had been punishment, according to the pastor. And just like there were mean men, like Georg and his father, there were also good ones, like Tata and Stefan. Konrad-Bátschi didn't fight, so he wasn't punished, whereas Stefan did and was.

But why? What terrible thing could Stefan have done that cost him three-quarters of his arm? *Or was the war not God's punishment at all?* she asked herself. Could Pastor Fröhlich be wrong?

ELISABETH STARED DOWN AT HER DRESS AND SHAWLS AS SHE approached her house. She couldn't hide this from Mammi but maybe she could at least change and make herself presentable again before telling Mammi what had happened.

Standing under the overhang that extended past the side wall of the house, Elisabeth peeked inside and, to her dismay, saw Mammi slicing cheese. Elisabeth thought about turning away and coming back later, but Mammi was already at the door. She opened it and immediately clapped her hands to her cheeks.

"By Jesus, Lissika, what happened?"

Elisabeth was angry at Georg but so confused by Stefan that the words again clumped in her throat, each story fighting to get out first.

"Don't stand there like a stupid cow. Come out of the cold, get changed, and tell me what happened. That will take forever to clean, if it comes clean at all."

Elisabeth stepped inside, removed her boots, lay her dirty shawls and mittens on the floor, and headed into the front room, closing the door behind her.

"Well?" Mammi called through the door.

Elisabeth drew the curtains and pulled out a fresh dress.

"Georg and Stefan walked over to me while the postman was delivering this week's news. I didn't want to be rude and walk away. After the postman had left, Georg had another one of his fits."

Elisabeth looked up at the crucifix. Why did she always find herself in such situations?

She caught her reflection in the looking glass and was horrified by her appearance: instead of wiping the mud off her cheek, she had smeared it over half her face and onto her blonde hair.

"Mammi, can you get some ash from the oven?" She took a rag usually used for polishing shoes and wiped the excess dirt off her face and then changed into her fresh dress, being careful to fold up the filthy one so that it wouldn't make anything else dirty.

"Good gracious, Lissika! What in heaven's name happened?"

Elisabeth could hear Mammi scraping around in the oven.

"Georg thought a child's ball was a grenade and pulled me and Stefan down to the ground to protect us."

"He what?!" Mammi slammed the oven's iron door shut.

Elisabeth buttoned up the front of her dress, pulled down on its skirt and sleeves, and took her braids out, letting her hair fall down her back and over her shoulders. She unfolded a fresh pair of woollen, striped socks and pulled them on. Then she slid into house shoes.

She added her dirty dress and socks to the laundry bag and then opened the door. "He believed he was at the front and that someone had thrown a grenade." Mammi had placed a pile of ash on a cloth and a jug of water next to the wash basin.

Mammi looked indignant. "A grenade? A child's ball?

Elisabeth, that is the most ridiculous thing I have ever heard. Even Luki can't make up that kind of story."

Elisabeth bent over the wash basin, throwing her hair into it. Mammi poured the cold water over her head, and she shivered as it ran down her scalp. Elisabeth splashed some of the water on to her face to remove the rest of the dirt while Mammi continued wetting her hair. "No, Mammi, it's true. He saw a ball coming at him and so he believed we were under attack and pulled me and Stefan down to protect us."

"From a child's ball?"

"Yes."

Mammi held the cloth with ash over a second water jug, poured water from the first one over it, and then used the tea in the second jug to rinse Elisabeth's hair. *And this is only the first thing I have to wash because of him*, Elisabeth thought.

"That man is being punished by God," Mammi said.

Even if the war had not been the punishment for millions of people, as Stefan had said, it certainly had been for Georg, a punishment he now relived daily. Not only had Mammi and Pastor Fröhlich said so, but Georg had, too. *He even said he deserved it*, she recalled.

"I know," Elisabeth said and renewed her promise to Jesus to not disobey her mother again.

CHAPTER ELEVEN

"Just a few more minutes," Meghan whispered to Juliana, whose mind kept drifting during geography class. It was Monday, a full week since Rachel's first panicked phone call and therefore almost a week since Kim's death. *Does Rachel count the days like this?* Juliana thought. *No, she probably counts the minutes.* She couldn't wait to text or talk with Rachel tonight: her best friend would be home from whatever weekend thing her father had taken her on.

"Here's your homework," Ms. Haseltine said as she wrote the instructions on the whiteboard. Juliana dutifully recorded them in her calendar on her phone and packed everything up. The bell rang and chairs screeched as everyone stood up to leave.

"How're you holding up?" Meghan asked as she, Juliana, and Shawna left the classroom.

"It's getting a little easier, but I'm still mad I couldn't fly back to Calgary to be with her."

Shawna, usually fairly quiet, spoke up. "I'm sure she missed you. It was tough a few years back when my dad died. My friends really helped me through it."

Juliana raised her eyebrows. "Oh, I didn't know. I'm sorry."

"It's all right. We knew it was coming—cancer. I imagine your friend is having a harder time than we did because her mom's death was so sudden. But I was glad to have the friends I did." She gave a smile to Meghan, who gave a bigger one in return. "I'm sure Rachel appreciates everything you tried to do from out here."

Juliana shrugged. "I don't know. I feel like it wasn't enough. I've never had to deal with this before, either. I never knew my dad's parents, my mom's mom died ten years ago...and I can't think of anyone else I know who's died. I mean, what do you do?"

They came upon a bank of lockers.

"Listen to the person whose family member has died," Shawna said. "Everyone keeps giving well-meaning but useless advice. It just ends up hurting you more because you really need to talk."

Juliana thought of the cake-baking suggestion she'd given Rachel when Kim was still on life support.

Shawna continued. "Just listen. If the person stops talking, ask a question—once—to encourage more talking. If they don't want to talk, they won't." She turned her back to Juliana and Meghan, suggesting the conversation was over.

Was that why Shawna was always so quiet? Was she still sad about her father's death? Would Rachel be that quiet for a few years, too?

"See you tomorrow," Meghan said, as though Shawna's behaviour was completely normal. Shawna nodded, though she didn't turn around.

"Yeah, see you," Juliana added, and followed Meghan to their lockers.

Meghan said, turning the dial on her lock, "When Shawna's dad was sick, I didn't know what to do either. And then when he died...I promised myself I wouldn't dump all my crap on her while she was going through all of that."

"I made that same promise, but it was really hard to keep."

Meghan opened her locker and packed her backpack. "I still needed someone to talk to. I was so thankful for my family and other friends Shawna and I had. It was like we'd somehow built a circle of support—we could help each other without burdening Shawna."

Juliana removed her lock and set it on the shelf in her locker. "That's what's happened to me." She told Meghan about how Aunt Anne had stepped in to help when her parents couldn't, and how talking with Opa and even Jasmine had made her feel better.

"It took me a while to see it," Meghan said, "but in hindsight, it was the best thing that came out of all of that: we all developed stronger friendships and bonds with each other." She slammed her locker shut and swung a gym bag over her shoulder. "Off to swimming!" she said.

As Juliana finished packing, the conversations with her two new school friends played over in her mind. First, she promised herself to do her best to listen to Rachel next time they talked. Second, she would be grateful to those who listened to her.

Juliana rang the doorbell at Aunt Anne's house.

"Hey," Charlie said, answering the door. He stepped back to let her in. "Mom, Juliana's here," he called into the kitchen.

Scott, only eight, zoomed out of the kitchen, a super hero in his hand.

"Pow! Pow! Pow!" he said.

To Juliana's surprise, Charlie feigned being shot and stumbled back against the wall. Scott raised his arms in victory, but Charlie pretended to struggle to find a gun in some pretend holster on his hip. Scott shot again and Charlie slumped down the wall.

"Pow! Pow! Pow!" Scott said to Juliana, but she stared at him.

"You're boring," he declared and ran up the stairs.

"Everything okay?" Aunt Anne shouted from the kitchen.

"Um, yeah," Juliana shouted back. "I just wanted to drop by. I can leave if—"

"Don't be silly! Come on in!"

Charlie, alive again, pointed the way to the kitchen, though Juliana already knew it, and disappeared up the stairs. "I've come back from the dead!" he shouted to his young brother.

"Everything okay?" Aunt Anne asked again as she came into the foyer, wiping her hands on a tea towel.

Juliana nodded, but now she felt awkward. She had come to say thank you? She couldn't have just called? Her aunt was obviously busy with cooking. "Yeah, everything's fine."

"Okay." Aunt Anne stared at her. "Well, it's nice to see you. Come on in." She turned to go back to the kitchen.

"Thanks. Um, Aunt Anne?"

"Mhm?"

"Thank you." Juliana slipped off her boots.

"Oh, I heard you."

"No, I mean thank you for, you know, last week. For inviting me over and all that."

Aunt Anne smiled. "You're welcome, though your mom

deserves some of the credit." Juliana had to agree, though rather reluctantly. "I'm home most days so you're welcome over anytime, always, but your mom knew you wouldn't just come by, so she asked me to call. Sorry—I've got a pot boiling. Come in and tell me how things are going."

Juliana followed her aunt and watched her fly around, from checking lasagna noodles on the stove to chopping up an onion on the kitchen island. *Kind of like Kim*, she remembered, and although part of her wanted to cry because she missed Rachel's mom, another part of her was happy at the memory. Was it possible to be happy and sad at the same time after someone died? Aunt Anne glanced up at her.

"You look puzzled," she said. "Anything I can help with?"

Juliana shook her head, feeling like she was intruding. She didn't want to bother her aunt with boring tales of high school and geography lessons. She had to think of something to get out of there and leave her alone.

"Is Sophie home?"

"She's upstairs doing math homework. I've been wanting to help her, but I can't get away from the kitchen. She wants to go skiing today still, so I'm trying to get supper done early."

"Could I help her? I got the math award in grade eight for my class. I'm sure I can help her with grade seven math."

Aunt Anne's face lit up. "Would you mind? Her room's

upstairs, second door on the left. I'll let Tata know you're here."

Juliana texted her parents to let them know where she was, set an alarm on her phone to make sure she'd get home in time to still do her work, and headed upstairs.

"I DON'T KNOW HOW I'M GOING TO LIVE WITHOUT HER," Rachel sobbed on the phone.

Juliana hadn't been home from dance for more than two minutes when her phone had rung and she had eagerly picked it up and dashed into her room. "I mean, she's not here anymore..."

Shawna's advice flew into Juliana's head, so she simply said, "I know."

"Sure I have my dad, but...he's my dad. I mean, what's he going to tell me about shaving my legs? Or waxing my bikini line by myself?"

"If you have the courage to do that," Juliana said with a chuckle. That was okay to say, wasn't it?

"True. But there won't be extra period supplies in the house, and I can't imagine asking any man to buy that stuff for me."

"Neither can I."

"It's not fair!" Rachel said. "Why my mother? Why did that bastard have to take my mother from me!"

Tears welled up in Juliana's eyes and her nose started to run. "I don't know, Rach." She grabbed a tissue and dabbed at her face.

Juliana wanted nothing more in this moment than to lock her friend in a caring embrace and tell her they were going to spend the night together and watch whatever movies and eat whatever food they wanted to. But that couldn't happen.

"You know what?" Juliana said when Rachel started to calm down, and then she stopped. Should she keep listening?

"What?"

"I'm sorry...did you want to say something else?"

Rachel sniffled. "To be honest, no. Not really. You go ahead."

Rachel's words sounded honest and not formal or polite, so Juliana continued. "I went to visit my aunt earlier today. The way she cooked in the kitchen reminded me of your mom. She had pots on the stove, she was chopping vegetables on the counter...just a blur in the kitchen." At first, Rachel didn't respond, and Juliana wondered if she had said something wrong. Maybe she shouldn't have spoken. "Rach?"

Rachel blew her nose and then answered. "When Dad and I were at this cabin near Lake Louise, it had a tiny kitchen with almost nothing in it, just the basics. Dad was really lost in there. You know him—if he doesn't have a million gadgets to cook with, he doesn't know what to do." She blew her nose again. "He admitted that Mom would know what to do, and then the two of us just started bawling." Rachel started crying again. "And it was like...it was like he hadn't stopped loving her."

Juliana couldn't hold her tears back either. The divorce had changed Rachel's life so dramatically that crying had become a regular occurrence for both of them for months. Even goofy movies couldn't get them to stop—the laughing eventually opened the floodgates.

Juliana yawned and looked at the time: it was 11:30. She had to get up in six and a half hours for school. In the moments of silence that followed, before either friend knew what to say next, the advice from everyone who had listened to Juliana came back, and she now realized that, even though different words were used, everyone had told her the same thing: she had to look after herself, too, because her life was moving forward. Juliana knew that, just like she had friends and family to help her through this week, so, too, had Rachel.

Now I see what Opa meant, she thought. Suddenly, the knowledge that Rachel had a circle of love to support her comforted Juliana. She could leave her now, and Rachel would somehow be okay.

Juliana yawned again. "Rach, listen—"

"You've gotta go?"

"Yeah, I'm really sorry."

"No, no, it's okay, Jules, really. You're my best friend and I'm so grateful for everything you've done."

"But what did I do? I mean, I wasn't at your mom's funeral. I can't have a sleepover with you or see you at dance..."

"It was great just to hear your voice."

That answer didn't sit right with Juliana. Was Rachel not telling her about others who had helped her? Juliana recalled the numerous offers of help on Rachel's social media feeds. *Not all of those would've been empty offers*, she thought. *Especially not from our dance team.* Juliana liked rules, guidelines, order. She didn't like not understanding where their friendship stood.

"I just want to ask you a question before we hang up, and you have to be honest with me, okay?" Juliana said.

A pause.

"Rach?"

"Okay, sure."

Juliana opened her mouth, but the question wouldn't come out. Truth be told, she was terrified of the answer. She knew that if she asked this question, and Rachel answered it honestly, or, at least the way Juliana thought would be honest, something was going to change.

"Jules?"

But she had to ask it, because Juliana and Rachel had to move forward, too. She took a deep breath. "Did your friends and family help you through this week? I mean, I know it was horrible, and I know 'sad' doesn't begin to describe how you feel, but did they get you through it?" Juliana's skin crawled with nervousness, and she began to feel queasy. But she needed to know the answer. "Rach? We're best friends. You have to be honest with me."

Another sob, and then Rachel answered. "They did, actually." Then she rushed to add, "But that doesn't mean that you—"

"It's okay," Juliana said gently. "Really, it's okay. It means you're surrounded by people who care about you and can help you, you know, work through this. Things have changed for us, and your mom's death has made that really clear to me."

Another pause. Time couldn't move any slower.

"Yeah. I know. I've felt it, too."

Both girls remained silent again, and Juliana let what they'd just admitted to each other sink in. In the midst of all this turmoil it had become clear that their friendship had changed. After Juliana and Rachel hung up, Juliana cried herself to sleep.

CHAPTER TWELVE

The next afternoon, Elisabeth ran out of the house quickly, leaving her siblings at home, so she could buy a few items before the weekend: gas and matches for their lanterns, and yeast and sugar for baking. Just as she stepped through the doorway of the tiny store, Georg walked out, his arms full with his purchases. He looked away, and Elisabeth was glad of it.

"Georg, hurry up." Konrad-Bátschi, his arms empty, followed his son out. He tipped his hat to Elisabeth, then headed for his horse and wagon, which had various farming tools in it. "We need to return Samuel's equipment to him and get back before sundown." Georg didn't respond and loaded his wares into the wagon

Elisabeth continued with her errands. She asked the shopkeeper for her wares, and the shopkeeper retrieved them and set them on the counter to tally them up. Elisabeth paid and thanked him. No sooner had she lifted her purchases off the counter than she heard a shout from outside.

"I've had enough of this!" It was Konrad-Bátschi.

She rushed out to see what was happening.

Georg's face was crushed in anger and he pushed at the air, as if pushing someone away. "I'll kill you!" he shouted.

Elisabeth gasped: Maria was right about Georg wanting to kill someone.

"You're humiliating our family name!" Konrad-Bátschi said. "There's no one there!"

Elisabeth could tell from Georg's eyes that he was somewhere else; he hadn't heard his father just like he hadn't heard Stefan the day before after he'd pulled them both to the ground. She scanned the crowd and saw a horrible mixture of finger-pointing, jeering, staring, and whispering. Thankfully, none of it appeared to be directed at her.

Just go home, she told herself. *This is his punishment from God. It's none of your business.*

Georg ducked from his invisible foe and swung again, reeling backwards as he retreated while defending himself. He crossed his arms in front of his face, knocking off his hat as he tried to protect himself from whatever or whoever he believed was attacking him.

"That's it, Georg! Get him!" a man shouted from the

crowd. The others laughed. A knot formed in Elisabeth's stomach. She couldn't help but keep watching.

Georg tripped and dropped onto the ground, causing more laughter from the ever-growing crowd. Shame and pity again arose in Elisabeth's heart, only this time, there was no anger.

Konrad-Bátschi threw his hat at his son. "Get up!" he shouted, but Georg continued protecting himself from his invisible adversary. "I said, get up!"

The more her uncle shouted at his son, the less Elisabeth could believe that God would punish Georg and not his father. She thought back to his sister's wedding when Georg had repeatedly said that Susi didn't deserve to die, even though there was no apparent threat on her life. He had asked Elisabeth why he'd had to watch his best friend die. And now recently, he had helped Elisabeth on several occasions. *He even put an end to his father's rude comments to me by getting the horse moving*, she thought. Clearly Georg was no longer the man who used to frighten children and pick fights with men. Wasn't the point of punishment to improve a person's behaviour? If so, then why would God continue punishing Georg if he had begun to change? Would it not make sense to stop these nightmares to help Georg be even nicer?

People moved in closer, pointing at Georg while they whispered to one another. Elisabeth recognized many of them. But Georg was oblivious to it all, pushing his pretend adversary off his chest and attempting to fire a pretend handgun.

"Oh, don't shoot me!" Meier Josef shouted out, his voice filled with mockery.

Konrad-Bátschi, the same size as Georg, pulled his son up onto his feet by his shirt. "Look at me!" he commanded, but Georg's eyes were still focused on the terror of the nightmare spreading through his body. His arms swung at his invisible foe. That his father stood in the way seemed irrelevant to Georg.

"I've worked my land to ensure I could pass it down to my eldest son and continue to provide for his family," Georg's father said. He punched his son in the stomach, knocking him back onto the ground. Elisabeth almost dropped her purchases. What father humiliated his own son this way? "And now it's going to go to waste once I die: you can't stay sane long enough to harvest one grain of wheat, and your lame brother can't walk more than the length of one street before he tires." He kicked his son and spat on him before turning his back and deserting him. To Elisabeth's disgust, several of the men patted her uncle's arm or shoulder as he passed them.

Elisabeth set her purchases down and took a step toward Georg and then hesitated: Mammi's shoemaking. They needed the money: they didn't have the income Georg's family did.

"Get up, Georg," Hagel Samuel shouted in a woman's

voice. "The dishes need to be washed!" The crowd roared with laughter.

Peter-Bátschi stuck his head out from the crowd. "There's a bomb coming, Georg!" he shouted.

"Bomb!" Georg yelled and threw himself down on the ground.

"Boom!" another man yelled.

"Ow!" cried out a different man.

"Andreas?" Georg looked up in fear, as though he was searching for someone.

Andreas was the name of one of Mammi's brothers who had died in the war. But then again, so many German Semlakers had the same name—Georg could've meant someone entirely different.

But he can hear us, Elisabeth realized. She didn't know why it was important, but only that Stefan had said the day before that it wasn't good when Georg couldn't hear.

The sounds of horses' hooves and rolling wagon wheels pulled her attention from her thoughts and she watched Konrad-Bátschi drive off, abandoning his son. She could only hope that Georg didn't hear that.

Peter-Bátschi strutted out in to the open. "Come on, Georg, shoot me! I'm your red enemy! Shoot me!"

Georg appeared to look for his gun.

"Can't find it?" Peter-Bátschi taunted. "Here it is!" He feigned throwing a weapon over Georg's head. Georg scrambled to his hands and knees and scurried after it.

He can hear and see us again, Elisabeth thought. *But what do I do now? And how can I help without starting more rumours about myself?*

The crowd kept teasing and belittling Georg. Elisabeth felt like she'd backed up against a wall.

Are we not supposed to help others? she asked Jesus. *These people are forcing him to relive something horrible instead of helping him. I want to help now, but if I do, I go against my mother's wishes, and our family will become poor. What do You want me to do?* Feeling completely helpless, all she could think of was her favourite prayer.

Our Father, who art in Heaven...

"I'm going to shoot you, Georg! Bang!"

...Hallowed be Thy name.

Georg's body snapped itself into a ball again, trying to protect itself from the shot.

Thy kingdom come,

Thy will be done...

"Stop it, all of you!" a man yelled.

Maybe God was listening to her prayers.

...on Earth as it is in heaven.

Stefan pushed through the crowd with his one arm. "You're all cowards for tormenting a helpless man!"

As Stefan stood between his friend and the crowd of tormentors, it finally made sense to Elisabeth: Jesus's will, which was also God's will, was to help, and since God was more important than her parents, Elisabeth was to obey Him first, and her parents second.

"I fought in the war—" a man said.

Stefan immediately interrupted him. "*I* fought in the war, too, and I spent two years in Russia afterwards. I didn't get to return to the comforts of my own home like the rest of you. Georg returned to a dead wife and baby after seeing countless other men die, including his best friend whom he'd promised to protect. I may not know what's happened here in the three years I've been gone, but I know none of you has spent as much time with wounded soldiers as I have. I'm telling you, this is happening to thousands, maybe tens of thousands of them!" He crouched down to Georg and whispered something in his ear. Georg's shouting stopped, but his body continued to shake.

Peter-Bátschi sauntered up to Stefan. "You were too stupid to escape. Another bomb, Georg!" When Georg curled up in to a ball, Elisabeth's uncle and the rest of the crowd roared again in laughter. Elisabeth thought she'd get sick to her stomach from all this cruelty.

Stefan jumped to his feet. "You drunken bastard! You think because you don't shake like your sister's nephew that you're fine? What goes through your head every night, eh? A man's eye getting pierced out?"

Elisabeth didn't know if she should cover her ears as Stefan's words turned into pictures in her mind.

Peter-Bátschi tugged at his own shirt collar. "Stop it."

"Body parts flying everywhere while your comrade lies on the ground, bleeding to death, begging you to help?"

Elisabeth's uncle passed his coat to Hagel Samuel and shook out his hands, preparing to fight. Elisabeth wiped away tears.

"The deaths of Adam and Andreas?" Stefan said, naming Mammi's two brothers who had also died.

"Andreas would still be alive if Georg had protected him as he had promised!" Peter-Bátschi took a swing at Stefan but lost his balance.

Elisabeth froze: Georg had promised to protect Mammi's brother? But the two families hated each other...

Stefan swung his leg to take out Peter-Bátschi's from underneath him, knocking Elisabeth's uncle to the ground.

Jesus, what do I do? she cried out in her mind. Her imagination created images she had never seen before. She began to feel just a grain of Georg's pain. But she also now understood why Mammi despised Tata's family so much, that it wasn't just their condescension she railed against.

"You think you're better than Georg because you use the bottle to control your nightmares?" Stefan shouted as Peter-Bátschi attempted to stand. "I know what goes through your mind every night, Peter. I may not have a gun or my shooting arm, but I have my memories, and they're the same as yours." He grabbed Mammi's brother by the shirt. "I won't hesitate to remind you of them if you don't leave Georg alone."

Then Stefan pushed him away, and the crowd began to quiet down. "We saw enough in Galicia," he said to Peter-Bátschi. "Let's not bring it back here. Move on. And let Georg at least try to move on."

Peter-Bátschi straightened his shirt and vest. "I'm not fighting you because it would be unfair," he said to Stefan. "You've only got one arm." He backed away, his chin held high. Hagel Samuel gave him his coat, and he put it on, buttoning it up.

As though the fight never happened, Elisabeth noticed.

Stefan turned to Georg, whose arms were wrapped around his knees like a scared child. "The war's over, Georg. You can go home."

Within a few moments, Georg's arms let go of his body, and he rolled onto his back, his head tipped to one side, and his eyes closed, as though he was sleeping. Elisabeth immediately recalled that Stefan had said similar words the day before and they had also ended Georg's shakes.

And that must have been what he said moments ago, she thought, *before my stupid uncle rekindled Georg's nightmare.*

"Just leave him be," Stefan said to everyone. "He's had to deal with enough bloodshed that he doesn't need to suffer at the hands of his own people, too."

Georg's body lay so still that Elisabeth had to look closely to be sure he was still breathing. His face was paler than the clouds floating overhead, and his eyes stared into nothingness.

"Go," Stefan said to them again. "It's Lent. Be kind to him."

One by one, people began to walk away, whispering to one another and looking over their shoulders as they headed to wherever they were going. Stefan kneeled beside Georg, and Elisabeth rushed over to join him. She understood now that, yes, she had to help, whether Mammi wanted her to or not. Not to do so went against Jesus's most basic teachings and God's will—even if Georg was responsible for Andreas-Bátschi's death. In other words, not helping would be a sin.

"How are you feeling?" Stefan asked, and Georg shook his head ever so slightly.

"What can I do?" Elisabeth wiped her tears.

Sorrow filled Stefan's eyes. "It looks like Georg was right. You're too young to hear these stories. I'm sorry. My anger was too strong."

"Body parts? Thousands of men?" she asked, tears rolling down her cheeks.

Stefan nodded.

"No wonder..." She looked with pity upon her cousin. "I remember the parades of soldiers heading off to war when I was young. I believed they wanted to go to war and that they would come back as heroes."

"That's what we all believed, at least at the beginning," Stefan replied. "By the time I had to do my military service, though, that had all changed. They just didn't tell anyone." He walked a few metres away to pick up Georg's hat and bring it back to him. Elisabeth now stared at Georg as though he, too, were missing an arm, so unfathomable to her was what she had just learned. Stefan continued. "When you're out there, prepared to do battle, you realize that your orders amount to one thing: to take another family's father, husband, brother. And to do that as many times as you can, knowing they have the same orders and would do the same to you. There's nothing heroic about that, no matter what side you're on." He turned his attention back to Georg. "Let me help you up."

Georg opened his eyes as Stefan held out his hand. Stefan was still so very thin from his years in a POW camp, and Elisabeth didn't know how he could hoist up with one arm a man twice his size. But Georg waved away Stefan's hand and slowly pushed himself up to his elbows and then his hands. The ground was drier today, but he was still covered in dirt and gravel.

The Lord's Prayer continued in Elisabeth's mind and she finally realized how she could help.

"Stefan, get Eva. Tell her that she and Georg are invited to my home for some bread and a little rest."

"No," Georg said. "Your mother would not—"

"I insist," Elisabeth replied, cutting him off. She would deal with Mammi afterwards. Right now, Georg's needs were more important than hers. "Go, Stefan, please. You'll be faster than me. Ask her to bring Georg some clean clothes."

Without saying a word, Stefan shot off to Konrad-Bátschi's house where Georg and Eva lived.

Georg raised himself to one knee and shook his head. "I know your mother wouldn't—"

"Shush. You can't go to Samuel's now. You're much too tired. And..." But she couldn't bring herself to say that his father had left.

"And Tata is already gone," he finished for her.

So he had heard his father leave. Her heart ached for him.

"I'm sorry," she said, brushing dirt from his shoulders. "And if you go home, Margarethe-Néni will...you won't be able to rest." She continued now to brush off his back. "Mammi will likely be in her workshop. I'll have to tell her you're visiting, but she won't be in the house." She quickly retrieved her purchases from the storefront entrance and then offered him her arm, though she didn't know if she could support his massive frame either. Georg did not need her help and they walked to Elisabeth's house, only a few short blocks away.

"Stefan cares a lot about you," she said as they walked. "You need more people like him to help you."

Georg said nothing, but his body said everything. His face was still ghostly white, and his gait was that of an old man, weary with age, and not that of the family heir, gifted blacksmith, and returned soldier.

"I am grateful for your kindness," he finally said, "but you're too young to understand, Lissika."

"I'm beginning to understand more, and my studies for my confirmation are helping, too."

"Then you know that we are punished for our sins. These shakes and nightmares are what happen to men who don't protect their friends." He looked in the direction of his home. "Or family."

CHAPTER THIRTEEN

"And?" Dad asked, his voice tinny on Juliana's phone. "How are things with Rachel?"

With the wind chill at -35°C, her hands protected in her mittens and tucked inside her pockets, Juliana was glad she'd remembered her earbuds this morning in case Dad called her on her way home from school.

"Okay, I guess," she replied, her breath visible in the air. Juliana didn't know how to describe what she was feeling. On the one hand, she was sad about the change in their friendship. On the other hand, something had shifted inside her, and she didn't feel as strong a longing to always contact Rachel. If she was to be honest with herself, she was beginning to enjoy spending time with her new friends. Although that made her feel like a traitor to her old ones, and especially to Rachel.

"I don't know if we're best friends anymore." Saying the statement out loud upset her, but not enough to cry.

"Distance doesn't make any kind of relationship easy. Your mom and I have worked really hard to raise you despite my being away all the time. And you and me, well, we've had difficulties too, over the years. But we're still a family."

"That's different. You always come back. I'll never go back to see Rachel."

"Just a sec. There's some idiot showing off his exotic car..."

Juliana held her breath, thinking of Kim and the accident. *Dad can't die now.* She let her breath out when she realized that he was the one in the transport truck. *He's braved some of the most dangerous passages through the Rockies,* she thought. *He can handle the highways here.*

"Sorry. Back again. Yes, you're right, there are differences. But the basics are still there: relationships are easier when you can see each other all the time. But if you have to deal with the distance, it does get easier. It never becomes easy, just easier."

Juliana checked both ways, crossed the street, took two steps on the opposite sidewalk, and lost her balance on a layer of black ice. "Why don't people clear their sidewalks?" she complained once she'd regained her footing.

"You okay?"

She sighed. "Yeah. Stupid ice. The freeze-thaw weather here is driving me insane. Sorry. You were saying?"

"When you were born, going back on the road was really, really hard. It's become easier over the years, but it's still not easy; I miss my family every time I leave. It's going to be like that for you and Rachel. I'm certain that the next time you see each other, it'll feel as though nothing's changed, and yet so much will have changed because you've both had to move forward. She'll make new friends and you're making new friends. But that doesn't mean you can't call each other or text or chat online. Right now it's just that the two of you haven't settled on what that new thing is yet."

Juliana had to admit that what Dad was saying sounded...okay actually. She had felt true happiness for Rachel when Rachel admitted that others had stepped in to help her. It meant she was being looked after and it wasn't Juliana's job to do that. Juliana still felt guilty about not being there for her, but acknowledging this change did feel like a bit of a relief.

"Jules?"

"Yeah, I'm here, just thinking."

"Did that make sense?"

"I think so. Listen, I'm at the door. I'll see you tonight, right?"

"If traffic goes well, I should be home by the time you

get back from dance. We can talk more if you want to: I'm home all weekend and Monday's Family Day here."

They said their goodbyes and hung up. Once Juliana entered the house, she sat down at the kitchen table and texted Rachel just to say hi.

I know you've got a lot to do and lots of people to help you, she wrote. *If you need me, you know where I am.* What else could she say? Have a good weekend? But her mom had just died. But that's also what normal people said. After thinking about it some more, she wrote, *This is going to sound dumb, but I don't mean it that way: if I don't hear from you, I hope you have a good weekend. Enjoy time with your dad. And...I'm sorry again about your mom.*

She grabbed herself an apple, and sat down, staring into nothingness as she ate, crunching and chewing. Her phone beeped.

Not dumb at all. Thank you. You're an awesome friend. I'll be busy for a while, but I will call you if I need anything.

Juliana quickly replied with a heart.

Opa, Mom, Dad, and Juliana sat around the kitchen table, enjoying sandwiches. Juliana hadn't heard from Rachel all weekend, and though part of her was sad, part of her again felt relieved.

"A penny for your thoughts?" Mom asked.

Dad and Opa looked up.

"Nothing," Juliana replied.

"Okay. But you haven't taken a bite in over a minute and you clearly look like you're somewhere else."

Juliana bit into her sandwich. "I'm fine," she said, her mouth somewhat full. One thing that had bothered her about this whole ordeal was that everyone kept asking how she was doing, as though they always expected her to share the next big emotion or something. Almost two weeks had passed since Kim's death, and Juliana was finally beginning to feel normal again. Could they drop it with the "how are you" and related questions?

Her phone beeped. She instinctively stood up, but Mom told her to sit back down. "We need to get back to normal rules," she said. "That means no phone during mealtime."

Juliana rolled her eyes. When her parents' phones went off during a meal, they got to answer. Why didn't she?

"Did you hear about the news with the rubber workers?" Opa asked. Mom nodded, Dad shook his head. "You should read up on it," Opa continued. "I'm not the only one who's lost co-workers to cancer."

Juliana raised an eyebrow. Opa had mentioned rubber workers before, and she knew he used to work at a local rubber factory, but that was it.

Mom caught her expression. "Things were unsafe for a lot of the workers at these factories, and people are saying that a lot more are dying from cancer than would be expected for any workplace. It's pretty scary, actually."

Opa pointed a finger at Mom. "You know Karl, right?"

"Of course, Tata. I've taken you to his place a few times."

Juliana had never met Opa's friend, but Opa often visited Karl at his house or saw him at the German club where he went to play cards, or talked to him on the phone. Opa and Karl were going to fly to Cuba with a seniors group the next week.

"Remember his cancer?"

Mom nodded again.

"They cured it a few years ago, but he's always worried it'll come back. That's no way to live. These companies should be forced to pay out for that."

Dad shrugged his shoulders. "Every job has work hazards that come with the territory. Look at mine." He pinched and shook his belly.

"Please don't," Juliana said.

Everyone laughed but then the conversation continued on about cancer and workplace health.

Can this conversation be any more depressing? she thought. Juliana ate her sandwich fast, gulped down her water, and left for her bedroom.

Belmont Village at 2? Jasmine had texted.

Juliana rushed back into the kitchen, interrupted to ask her parents if she could go, and did a little jump when they said yes.

"It's good you're going out with new people," Mom said.

Juliana had to agree.

"IT'S GREAT TO GET OUT," JULIANA SAID. SHE CUT OFF A piece of her chocolate cake and popped it in her mouth. "At lunch they started talking about cancer and getting health problems from work."

Jasmine scrunched up her nose. "Old people's talk." She had chosen a fruit flan with whipped cream.

"But my parents are only in their forties!"

"Old people's talk," Jasmine repeated and both laughed.

Remembering Meghan's advice from last week, Juliana said, "You know, I owe you a thank you. You've been great to have around during all of this."

Jasmine drank a sip of peppermint tea before answering. "Life's been pretty unfair to you lately. My parents always have to be there for others so I guess that's rubbed off on me a bit."

Juliana liked this café: it had a bit of a 1950s appeal to it, with a pink, black, white, and chrome colour scheme. But the tables and chairs looked thoroughly modern: clean, simple lines. Orderly, just how Juliana liked things. "You know," Juliana said, "I've been so busy these past few weeks talking about my family and all that I've never asked about yours. I mean, I was at your house once, but your parents weren't home. Your grandparents came from Guatemala? But Filopovic?"

"My mom's parents. My dad's parents are from Yugoslavia. Well, Serbia, but it was Yugoslavia when they were born. But I don't talk about my parents much. There's not much I can share."

Juliana sensed something uncomfortable but she was afraid to ask anything else. The last thing she needed was to dig up more sad news. At the same time, if Jasmine wanted to talk about something...

"Not really," Jasmine said when Juliana asked. "Mom's an operating room nurse. My dad's with the regional police. They see the worst of the worst, so I just try not to be a bother to them."

Juliana let out a snort and felt immediately embarrassed by her inappropriate reaction. "I'm sorry," she said, still smiling. "I was just thinking I'm pretty sure I do everything possible to be a bother to mine."

Jasmine giggled. "Okay, I have to admit, that is funny." She ate another bite of her flan. "All joking aside, though, you've got it really nice. Spend time with your grandfather. I know dealing with dementia can be hard but he's your only connection to the past. And to that book."

Juliana sighed and picked at her piece of cake. "I know. I try not to think about it, though."

Jasmine looked directly at Juliana. "If you want to know everything you can about that book, now's the time to do it. He'll only forget more and more."

CHAPTER FOURTEEN

"What?" Mammi said and stood up, her nostrils flaring.

"Georg and Eva are here," Elisabeth repeated. "He needs to rest, but he can't go home right now. He had another shaking episode." She took one step out the door of the workshop, but it wasn't fast enough to avoid whatever Mammi was going to say next.

"Are you trying to cost me business and terrify your siblings?" she shouted. Her face turned red and her gaze pierced Elisabeth.

"Mammi, you should've seen him—"

"Peter was already over to tell me. I don't need to see Georg and I certainly don't need him in my house!"

Elisabeth stared at the floor and twisted her hands. How could she explain this?

"He deserves all that ridicule," Mammi said. "Georg never was a good man—always just like his father—and now he's being punished for it. If God would only punish his father in the same way, I would be even happier."

"But that's just it, Mammi," Elisabeth said. "Why isn't God punishing Konrad-Bátschi? If they were both horrible to our family, then why one and not the other?"

Mammi glared at Elisabeth. "Because Georg allowed my brother to be killed."

How could Elisabeth ask her mother to forgive Georg for that? If someone had promised to protect any of her siblings and had failed, could Elisabeth truly forgive such a sin? Elisabeth didn't know. All she knew was that Georg needed her help, and her family needed his family's help. Maybe if Mammi knew what he had said, it might change her mind.

"He feels guilty for not having saved Andreas-Bátschi. I'm certain that's partly what's tormenting him so much. If you would just ask him about it—"

"Have you forgiven the Hagels? That's what you're really asking me to do, isn't it? Forgive Georg?" She returned to her sewing.

The question caught Elisabeth off guard. The Hagels—Samuel and his son, Konrad—had been asked to help repair the pigs' stalls. It had ended in a disaster and could've been worse if Georg and Stefan hadn't shown up to help. But the Hagels had also treated Luki poorly, and at one point, Elisabeth had feared they had hit him. She had become angrier at Hagel Samuel when she had seen how he had acted yesterday, after Georg had pulled her and Stefan down into the mud. Elisabeth was also certain the Hagels had begun those rumours about her.

"I guess I'm still angry at both of them," she confessed.

"You are young, hopeful, and naive, Lissika," Mammi said, looking up again. "But you are also old enough now to hear the story about my brothers and Georg. When we got news that Adam had died, Modr was beside herself. You were not quite ten. Georg mocked our family and said Adam simply hadn't protected himself enough. Later, when Andreas and Georg were drafted, Georg boasted that only true men would survive the war. He declared that since Andreas came from such 'poor stock' as he called us, he would protect him."

"But Mammi, clearly he didn't know what he was saying."

"Do not interrupt me!"

Elisabeth fell silent.

"But things changed. Andreas wrote home several times, and to all our surprise, he and Georg had become very good friends. Both men wrote about how much they treasured one another, and once, Georg wrote to his father that he would indeed protect Andreas, with his life if necessary. Konrad-Bátschi and Magarethe-Néni let us know how angry his intentions made them."

Elisabeth never knew that her uncle and cousin had developed such a strong bond. She understood better now why Georg made Mammi so angry.

Mammi picked up her sewing. "And that such a liar has come home and not my brother...You will learn that forgiveness is hard to give. Georg has the flames of Satan burning inside him, Elisabeth. Stay away from him unless you want them in you, too."

Elisabeth shook her head. "I believe Jesus is trying to pull the Devil out," she said. "Georg has been kind to us on several occasions. Is it not possible to assume that he has seen the light of Jesus, but that this war has exposed him to the Devil? The Devil cannot fight with himself, as Pastor Fröhlich said on Sunday."

Mammi's hands stopped moving, and Elisabeth knew she had her attention. "Only Jesus can fight the Devil. I believe the fire inside Georg is of Jesus trying to fill him, but the Devil is trying hard to keep hold of him."

Mammi resumed her work. "If you are right, if these are demons in his head and not a punishment from God, mark my words, Elisabeth: when these demons are gone from his head, he will be as he was." Mammi tied a knot and cut the thread. "You can talk to Pastor Fröhlich at your next confirmation lesson. I'm certain he will agree with me." She sighed. "But your cousins are here, and people have seen them come. They may stay but not long. Tell them I'm too busy to visit with them and tell me when they have left."

That was Mammi's way of saying she agreed—though maybe only a little—with Elisabeth. Elisabeth thanked her, retrieved some cheese and a jar of pickles from the root cellar, and returned to the house.

There she saw all three siblings—with Anna in the middle—huddled under the kitchen table.

"What are you doing under there?"

Their gaze into the front room answered her question.

"Why don't you three go outside," she said. "You haven't had any fresh air this afternoon." It was the best excuse Elisabeth could come up with that didn't further insult Georg. "Come back when the sun starts to set."

Without any argument, the children scrambled from under the table and disappeared into the back room to get their outdoor clothing.

Georg had changed into the clothing Eva had brought along and was now smoking a cigarette. Some colour had returned to his face. Once she had put on her house shoes, Elisabeth offered apologies from her mother and grabbed a dish for his ashes.

"I understand," Georg said, and Elisabeth could tell by the tone in his quiet voice that he knew why. She asked everyone what they wanted to eat.

"Oh, nothing," Eva said, trying to be polite. "We're grateful to just be away from prying eyes."

Elisabeth had never seen Eva like this. In the past, Georg's young wife had always greeted her loudly, as though she hadn't seen them in years. In fact, everything with her was loud, so much so that Elisabeth dreaded visiting her every time she was invited over. She had only done so now because Eva was Georg's wife and it was the right thing to do.

But now, Eva sat before Elisabeth, quiet and still. *Maybe embarrassed?* Elisabeth wondered. After what had happened to Elisabeth yesterday, she could empathize. *Eva deals with this every day*, she thought.

"No," she said. "You must eat something. I can tell by your face that you're tired, Georg. Even a little bread and butter will help you. But I also have cheese and pickles. That should give you a little more energy." It was, after all, the reason she had invited them over in the first place.

They accepted her offer and Elisabeth immediately headed into the kitchen. She pulled out three plates from the cupboard. When she turned around, Eva was standing by the table, holding a pair of women's shoes in her hands. She turned them over.

"These need new soles," she said. "Would your mother be willing to repair them?"

Elisabeth accepted the shoes. "Thank you. I will ask."

"Will this be enough?" Eva pulled out of her small purse the same amount Elisabeth had paid the midwife.

Elisabeth was certain Mammi didn't charge this much. She began to protest but Eva insisted.

"You have been more than kind," Eva said.

Elisabeth accepted the shoes and money. "I'll be sure to give these to Mammi later," she promised and set them and the money on her bed in the front room.

"Thank you," she said to Georg. He nodded again and took a puff on his cigarette.

Elisabeth returned to the kitchen and began slicing bread. Eva followed her.

"Stefan told me on the way over here what had happened," Eva said quietly. "Living with Mammi and Tata is becoming more difficult, so I'm—we're—grateful that you've invited us to your home." She glanced over her shoulder at Georg. Elisabeth followed her gaze. He now held his cigarette in his mouth while he paged through one of Tata's encyclopedia books. "To be honest," Eva continued, "Tata is becoming increasingly harsh with him. He yells at him every day. If it's not about his shaking, it's about how poorly he can support us and how he's become a burden to his family."

Elisabeth shook her head in dismay. "The war changed the men in many ways, didn't it?" For a moment, she felt some sympathy for her uncle: the son who returned was not the son who had left. But her sympathy lasted only for a moment. As the images of her uncle humiliating his helpless son replayed in her mind, her anger returned. She cut some cheese from the round and placed the pieces on each of the plates.

Eva rubbed her stomach. "I must tell you something, Lissika, because you're the only one of us I trust. Stefan has been very kind to Georg, but he's a man, and Georg's sisters are, well, I don't feel close to them."

As much as Elisabeth appreciated the compliment, she knew it would make things more difficult with Mammi, so she chose instead to say nothing and twisted open the jar of pickles and asked Eva to reach her a fork.

"Georg and Stefan told me about the...problems between your family and mine," Eva said, as she obliged. "I hope we can mend those wounds."

Elisabeth stopped and looked up at her cousin. She did not know this side of her, but Elisabeth had to admit that it was pleasant.

"You're not saying much," Eva remarked.

Elisabeth speared a pickle and shook off the excess liquid. She glanced back at Georg, who appeared engrossed in whatever he was reading.

"I didn't know until today that Georg was responsible for Andreas-Bátschi's death," she said.

"Oh! But it's not like that!" Eva said. "Stefan and Georg told me everything. Georg, come here." He glanced up from his book but remained seated. "You have to tell Lissika about her uncle."

Fear arose on his face, and Elisabeth worried he might

succumb to another episode. As much as she wanted to hear what he had to say, it had become clear that discussing the war disturbed him too much. "It's all right," she said and brought him his food. "The war's over. Let's talk about something else." In her mind, she had forgiven him: he had paid enough.

Eva nodded in agreement and Georg immediately relaxed. He inhaled his cigarette and blew the smoke out, away from the young women.

That's right, Elisabeth thought. *The great war is over.* She recalled Stefan's words to the crowd: *Move on.*

"But may I share our good news?" Eva asked. He nodded. She smiled at Elisabeth and placed her hand on her dress again. "We're expecting our first baby."

Knowing what Mammi was going through, and now understanding Georg a little better, Elisabeth didn't know if this was good news or not, though it should have been.

"That's wonderful," she said.

Eva took hold of Elisabeth's hands and forced her to face her. "I'm tired of pretending like everything's all right," she said, "I'd like you to stop pretending in front of us, too. You've seen my husband at his worst, Lissika. There's nothing left to hide."

Had Eva always been so loud and annoyingly happy because she was pretending that she and Georg were doing fine?

Georg crunched away on a pickle.

Elisabeth returned to the kitchen, and Eva followed her. She picked up the other two plates, but when she turned around to go back, she saw that Eva's eyes had turned red and she was blinking back tears. Elisabeth set the plates back down.

"You're the only woman I can talk to about him," Eva said as she dried her eyes and tried to regain her composure. "Did you see his reaction there?" Elisabeth nodded. "It's like he doesn't care, and I'm terrified this child will have these same fits," Eva said.

"Let's eat out here," Elisabeth said. "I wonder if Georg just wants to be alone for a little while." She peeked over Eva's shoulder. Georg appeared to again have lost himself in the book, puffing away on his cigarette. "He looks very content right now," she added. Both sat down and began to eat.

"I've been thinking a lot about him," she said, and she explained to Eva everything: from her fears about Georg being punished by God to disobeying her parents to Pastor Fröhlich's sermon. Eva sat, riveted, hardly eating as she listened. "Georg is...I don't know what you would call it... perhaps 'broken' is a good word, because of the war," Elisabeth said when she had finished. "Your baby will not see that kind of war. So I don't think you have to worry about that." She bit into a soft piece of bread.

Eva rested her chin on her hand and appeared to be

reflecting on what Elisabeth had said. "Do you really think so?"

"Nothing else makes any sense, Eva."

Eva smiled and turned toward Georg who appeared oblivious to their conversation. Elisabeth could feel warmth filling her chest. Was this what it meant to truly do God's will?

CHAPTER FIFTEEN

Juliana let her backpack fall onto the floor. "I got my report card."

"Give it here," Mom said. "It can't be that bad."

"Wanna bet?" Juliana dumped her bag onto the floor and picked up a crumpled ball of paper.

"Juliana!" Mom scolded. "We probably have to sign that!"

"So what?"

Dad moved over to Mom while she flattened out the report card. He studied the marks.

"Seventy-nine?" he said incredulously. "You're upset over a seventy-nine?"

"This month couldn't be any worse," she said and began bawling.

"You're not helping," Mom whispered to Dad. "She's been through a lot."

"I barely graduated high school," he replied. "I would've rejoiced with a seventy-nine."

"She's not you."

Mom put her arm around Juliana and pulled her daughter into a hug. Dad patted her on the back and apologized for his comment.

"We're not perfect," he said. "We don't expect you to be perfect, either."

Mom guided Juliana to a chair, and Dad handed her a box of tissues and a glass of water.

"You tried your best," Mom said. "You can't expect more of yourself than this."

"It's because of this stupid move! If we'd stayed at home, I'd have my marks!" Anger filled her. "Life was fine back home. This isn't fair."

"Dementia isn't fair," Dad said, his voice tense. "Life isn't fair."

"You're not helping," Mom said again.

"But she needs to keep things in perspective. Rachel just lost her mother, and we're talking marks here. Juliana's still got three-and-a-half years to go. Marks aren't that important."

Mom parked her hands on her hips and shot Dad a look.

Juliana stamped her foot on the floor and stood up.

"They were the only thing I had left from home that I thought wouldn't change!"

She went to her room, pulled out her book of goals for the year and opened it up to the first page.

✓ Get my splits

✓ Bend my back in half

✓ Make and keep 5 new friends in January

✓ Maintain 90% average at new school

✓ Raise competition average from 85% to 95%

There was no way she was going to maintain that academic average now. She'd have to get nearly a hundred percent on everything this semester to bring that up. She tore out the page, crumpled it into a ball, and threw it at her window. She then tossed her book to the other side of her tiny room.

There was a knock at the door. It was Mom. She sat down in Juliana's office chair.

"Your dad's just trying to give you some perspective, that's all," she said calmly. "He's had a different life than the two of us have. But I explained to him that it's not just the marks."

Juliana pulled her knees up to her chin and wrapped her arms around them. She wasn't in the mood to talk.

"You're right: this move has been a lot harder on you than any of us could have anticipated." That was what Mom wanted to say? Wasn't it pretty obvious already? "And then with Kim passing, and now your marks. And I imagine you're nervous about your first competition tomorrow. Am I right?"

Juliana nodded.

"What's this?" Mom asked and reached for Omama's notebook on Juliana's night table. Juliana had forgotten to put it away the night before.

"Opa says to not touch the drawings. They'll smudge," Juliana mumbled.

Mom leafed through them and repeated her question.

"Omama's drawings," Juliana answered. "You haven't seen them?"

"What?" Mom's face filled with surprise. "Tata's mom? No..."

Juliana explained the whole story. "I guess I assumed you knew. Sorry."

"Your father had told me about a book of drawings, but I somehow didn't get he meant this. Modr had taken up painting in her later years, but...to be honest, they were horrible. Even Tata agreed to throw most of them out after she'd died. Wait..." Mom kept paging through. "No, I think Tata did tell me about this once, but when I was really young, maybe in grade one or two. That's all I remember."

Juliana reached out for the book and Mom passed it back to her. She opened it to the drawing of the lantern.

"They didn't have electricity back then," Mom said. "Tata told me that the Germans in the village didn't connect to the electrical line that had been installed between the wars until after the Second World War. But why would she draw an everyday object? Just to practise?"

Juliana shook her head. "That's what I thought at first, too. But I think she was maybe angry about something. At least, that's what Jasmine and I thought once we looked at it. That flame looks like it's about to burst, but it's contained by that glass." She flipped back a few pages. "But there's more. Look here...hands pulling off mittens, a wedding party." She jumped ahead a number of pages and showed Mom the drawing of the funeral.

Mom shuddered. "I don't know why pictures of dead people were so important to them. I remember Tata getting photos when I was young of dead people. Yuck."

Normally, Juliana would have agreed with Mom. But since her discussion with Opa, she'd changed her mind. "To be honest, I really wished I could watch Kim's funeral. I feel like I missed out on something so important. Maybe these pictures were about that."

"I can see that, but Kim's casket would have probably been closed. Those pictures clearly showed the dead person."

Juliana couldn't help but wonder if those photos were perhaps in the basement. She would look later.

"But other things in here are just normal things," Mom said, "like that envelope...the kitchen..." She jumped farther ahead. "A barn...Oh, what's this?" Mom stopped at a drawing of a man with part of his arm missing—it had been cut off above the elbow. His other arm was around another man who was almost twice his size. The first man was smiling, but the second one only a little.

Juliana recognized the larger man.

"Wait..." she said and paged back to the wedding and then the funeral, flipping between all three drawings a few times. "I think that's Georg again."

Mom said nothing for a few moments then shook her head. "No, doesn't ring a bell."

"Opa said he wasn't a man, that he didn't look after his family. Like that's all a man's capable of doing," she said, criticizing Opa. "I mean, this guy fought in a war! The more Opa talked about him, the more I think he had PTSD. Isn't that mean to say about him?"

Mom shook her head. "I doubt that's what he meant. You have to remember, back then people didn't like you if your house wasn't clean enough. It was ridiculous. But turn back to that lantern."

Juliana sighed. At least Dad was on her side on this one. But now was not the time to discuss it. She turned the page to the lantern.

"It's mesmerizing somehow, isn't it?" Mom asked. "And she was only fourteen?"

"Yeah. To be honest, it's how I felt at dance on Saturday. Like this energy was burning inside me but it was somehow contained. Miss Denise said she'd never seen me dance so well before."

Mom shook her head in disbelief. "All the things I miss because I'm at work all the time."

Yeah, Juliana thought. *Exactly.*

"It sounds like you found the zone," Mom said. Juliana asked what she meant. "It's when you're in this place of flow where energy just, I don't know, runs through you in a really directed way. Your brain's firing on all cylinders, your concentration is really good, and everything, I don't know, it just flows."

"Yeah, that's it. But I was so angry...I've never been that angry before when I've danced."

Mom looked thoughtful. "Maybe it opened the flow for you." She moved over to Juliana's bed and took her hand. "Your father and I are really sorry that this move has been this hard on you. But we're grateful you have dance to help you deal with some of it. Tell me more about what you feel when you dance."

As words leapt out of Juliana's mouth—"freedom," "anger," "happy," "power"—her legs began to relax and her shoulders drop. Mom let go of her hand but pulled up one leg onto the bed so she could face Juliana square on. The more Juliana talked, the more animated she became, and the more she smiled. Yes, something had definitely changed inside, and even though she didn't fully understand it, she knew it was something good.

CHAPTER SIXTEEN

March 12, 1920

Dear Tata,

Thank you for your postcard. It was a wonderful surprise! We were all very happy to hear from you.

I wish I could write you and say that I am doing well, but I am not. I have been studying hard for my confirmation, but there are some things I cannot figure out. They have to do with your family.

Elisabeth paused. She had spent every moment since Georg and Eva had left praying for an answer to her question: how could she feel good about helping Georg and Eva when it meant disobeying her mother? She understood God's will was more important, but she had to acknowledge that she had to live in this house until she married. How did God want that to work? Not getting an answer, she decided to write Tata: he would know. But how much did she want to tell him? Did she have to admit that Mammi forbade her from passing on his greetings?

She stared at the paper. With everything that had gone on these past two weeks, she needed to talk to someone about it, but the only person she trusted with this was her father. At the same time, she didn't want to worry him either. She took a deep breath and wrote slowly.

You know that Georg succumbs to these horrific fits. I've seen them now, and I'm greatly troubled. Before you left, you told me to be strong and do what Jesus would want me to do. But I don't know what that is.

God wants me to obey my parents and to help and forgive our fellow man. Mammi forbids me from helping Georg, but when I help him, I feel warm inside. I believe I'm doing God's will: what tormented soul does not benefit from friendship?

But I now know about Georg's promise to protect Andreas-Bátschi. That must make Mammi very angry, and I understand why she dislikes your family so much.

But he and Samuel and a friend, Stefan Schäfer, have helped us several times now. I know Mammi has a brother and several brothers-in-law, but Peter-Bátschi takes to the bottle now and can be—

"What are you doing?"

Elisabeth jumped at Luki's interruption. She instinctively placed her hand over her letter. "None of your business," she said.

"Thank...you...for..." he began reading through her fingers. "See? I've been doing my homework."

"This is not the time to use what you've learned. Now leave me alone."

A mischievous smile crept over Luki's face, and Elisabeth knew that if she didn't do something soon, he would steal the letter from her. The encyclopedia Georg had been reading from still lay open on the table. Elisabeth had planned to read it herself and see what had interested him so much after she ironed her dress and wrote her letter to Tata.

"A friend...Stefan..." Luki read, his grin getting bigger. "Do you like him?"

"Luki, that's enough," Elisabeth said. She placed the letter inside the encyclopedia, slammed the book shut and returned it to its place on the shelf where Luki couldn't reach.

"That's not fair!"

"It's rude to read someone else's private thoughts. Now, go back outside and play."

"I came in for some water." Walking like the man he was trying to be, Luki strutted into the kitchen and helped himself to a cup.

Elisabeth rolled her eyes. "I might as well feed the animals and prepare for supper," she said to herself. She couldn't risk continuing the letter so long as Luki was here, and if Mammi showed up...she would finish it later.

Luki ran back outside. Elisabeth put on her boots and wrapped an old but warm shawl around her shoulders. Out in the poultry yard, she grabbed a bucket, filled it with dried corn kernels, and spread them out all over the ground in the duck house.

Footsteps down the street drew her attention, and she and her neighbours waved to each other. Elisabeth then continued to feed the geese and chickens.

"Oh, Luki," she said when she noticed that he had forgotten to close the gate behind him. As she approached the gate, she saw Stefan walking down the street with the other former prisoner of war who had returned with him. Stefan waved to Elisabeth, appeared to say something to his companion, and then jogged over while his companion continued on his way.

Stefan entered the yard and tipped his hat. "I'm glad to see you," he said. "There is something I need to talk to you about."

Elisabeth pulled her shawl tighter around her shoulders: it was cooler outside than she had expected. Stefan noticed and promised he wouldn't keep her long. "I wanted to thank you for your help with your cousin."

Elisabeth's eyes, apparently living a life of their own

whenever Stefan was around, again stared at his missing arm.

"Enough!" she said out loud. Her cheeks burning, she apologized to Stefan.

"It's all right." Stefan lifted his stump. "I'm also not used to being the only one around without a complete body. Trust me. You're not the only one who stares."

Elisabeth allowed herself to look at his arm now that Stefan was moving it around and looking at it himself. "The war hurt many men, didn't it?"

He ran his hand down the upper half of his arm and cupped its end in his palm. "I prefer the word 'broke,'" he said. "'Hurt' is too nice. But that's partly why I wanted to speak with you." He dropped his hand to his side and Elisabeth raised her eyes to look at his. His expression became dark. "Georg's mind is broken, and I don't know if it will ever get better. That means I also don't know if people will ever change how they treat him. But you actually talk to him. When we met on the road that one day—you were returning from the store and we were headed there—and he just nodded to you when we said our goodbyes. You didn't shout at him, or roll your eyes, or anything like that. You accepted his gesture. I thought that was very kind."

As nice as Stefan's compliments were, they made Elisabeth uncomfortable, because they only told half the story. *Must I tell him?* she asked Jesus. In her heart, she heard *yes.* Elisabeth sighed, wishing Jesus had answered other prayers of hers rather than this one. She played with the ends of her shawl. "Thank you, but please don't think so highly of me."

Stefan cocked his head to one side, and Elisabeth cast her eyes to the ground. Gradually she recounted to Stefan how she had at first felt sorry for Georg but then believed he was being punished and that he was possibly plotting to take revenge on those who mocked him.

"What?" Stefan said to her last idea. She immediately felt embarrassed for how she had acted. "Georg is incapable of killing anyone, Elisabeth. *That's* his problem. Yes, he was a bull before, but even then, he could never kill anyone." He paused, stunned by what she had said. "People obviously still don't understand war. You either shoot or are shot. If you shoot, you might survive. If you don't, you die. He believed he had a wife and young child here waiting for him to come home. And no one told him the truth. He was still on the front when I began fighting, Elisabeth. His nightmares had already begun, but believing he had a family at home gave him hope to survive."

"And my uncle?" The question had escaped before Elisabeth could catch it. "Mammi blames Georg—"

"I know. Georg blames himself, too. Georg says he and your uncle had been separated by command. He begged to fight alongside Andreas to protect him, but his request was denied. Hours later, when Georg couldn't find Andreas among the men who'd returned, he searched for him in the field infirmary. I'll spare you the details, but I can say that your uncle was breathing but unconscious. He died not much later." Stefan stopped. "Georg's nightmares are a mix of events, but many of them recreate in his mind what he believes he would've done had he been able to fight alongside your uncle." He placed his hat back on his head and sighed.

"My God..." Elisabeth said. The anguish Georg must have felt now twisted her gut and she placed her hand over her stomach.

"I'm so sorry," he said. "I wish we could talk about something more pleasant. But I need people to know what we saw. I think that would help them understand him better and maybe even respect him a little."

Elisabeth took a few breaths and prayed for help. "I can barely listen to what you've said just today, and yet you and all the other men *lived* this every day."

"And Georg for several years."

"You all see this in your dreams." That also meant Peter-Bátschi. It was no wonder he drank alcohol to soothe them. *Omama would not understand*, she thought. She lowered her hand. "But you bring him out of it. How?"

Stefan shook his head. "I only help it end faster. It was something I learned in Russia that seemed to work with some men, and certainly not all the time. But a reminder that they could return home often seemed to comfort them. Georg has to be able to hear me, though. When he's engulfed in a nightmare, nothing can reach him." Stefan glanced toward Elisabeth's house. "Georg tells me you are now, in a sense, the mother of this house. I'm sure you have many duties to tend to. But there is one last thing I must still tell you." He tucked his hand in his pocket and looked around him to see if anyone was near.

He lowered his voice. "Eva brought him to my house after they left here: she couldn't bear to take him home yet. As soon as he came in, he began to cry. Not because of a nightmare but because no one in his family has shown him as much kindness as you have."

Elisabeth's hand flew to her heart. She was expecting Stefan to share another one of Georg's shaking fits, or perhaps to say something about Konrad-Bátschi. This revelation surprised her, and the warmth Elisabeth had felt earlier returned. Had her actions truly meant so much? Just by offering him some bread?

"Thank you," she said. "But I changed my mind in part because of how you stood up to everyone."

"And I acted because I believe that God wants us to help others wherever we can." He paused for a moment, as if unsure about what he wanted to say next. "If I can make just one request, Elisabeth: please promise me you'll stop doubting Georg. Believe me when I say he's terrified. The war has not ended for him and he can't escape it. But maybe with some friends to help him, he might find some relief."

Elisabeth's heart beat fast in her chest. If she promised to help Georg, she would be going expressly against the wishes of Mammi. But that warmth continued to grow. She knew helping Georg was the right thing to do, just like calling the midwife had been the right decision. She would have to trust that Jesus would show her the way through the struggle she was about to create for herself.

"I promise," she said to Stefan.

He smiled. "Thank you."

Elisabeth closed the gate behind him. Once she was back in the house, though, she remembered her letter and then slapped herself on the forehead. "I didn't pay attention to what book I put the letter in!"

But it didn't matter anymore. She no longer needed to ask Tata what she should do. She would simply start a new letter and tell him about what she had done.

IT WAS A BEAUTIFUL, COOL SUNDAY HALFWAY THROUGH March: the fourth Sunday of Lent. With the service over, all the congregants had spilled out of their small, yellow church and onto the churchyard and surrounding areas to talk and gossip. Anna, Luki, and Rosina had found their friends and were running around the yard with them. Mammi was talking with Peter-Bátschi, Sophie-Néni, and Omama when she glanced over and saw who Elisabeth was with. The expression on her face said she disapproved, but that was better than one that said she forbade Elisabeth from talking to Tata's family. Although Mammi had done nothing but complain about the shoes and how Tata's "horrible family" was again forcing her to do work for them, her tone had softened. Eva's gesture had opened the door, Elisabeth realized.

"A beautiful day, isn't it?" Stefan said.

Elisabeth had to agree with him.

"Spring is finally around the corner, it seems," Eva said.

"And with it, planting season," Samuel added.

In his slow, monotone voice, Georg said, "Do you need more help on your farm?"

"Yes," Elisabeth said. "I know our land is small compared to yours, but I don't know how I'm going to manage everything. I can't take Anna and Luki out of school to help, and Rosina will only be able to do so much. Mammi is much slower at making shoes than Tata, so I don't know how often she'll be out." Elisabeth didn't mention the baby.

Samuel glanced at Georg, and Georg nodded. "It's a good thing your land is next to ours," Samuel said. "I'm certain we can find a way to help you. Is there anything else?"

"Actually, I do have one more request," Elisabeth said. The midwife had complained about the drafts in Tata's workshop. If Mammi was going to continue working in there, she needed a source of heat to help her stay healthy. "Could you build a small heating stove in the workshop? I know spring is coming, but Mammi works some evenings, and it can get cool in there. Nothing very big. Something where she could leave the door open for light but still feel warm?"

Samuel looked at his older brother again, but Georg didn't immediately respond. Elisabeth worried she had asked too much.

"Does Lissa-Néni want me to do this?" Georg finally asked.

"I'll make sure she does," Elisabeth said.

Georg let out a little chuckle and she wondered what was so funny that it actually caused a reaction.

"You are naive, Lissika," Georg said. *The third time someone's said that in a week*, she noticed with mild annoyance. She was already fourteen. When would that comment stop? "But it's nice to see such confidence. When your mother has approved it, I will."

"Might I be of use?" Stefan asked.

The question hung in the air like the moment when a gangly boy asks a beautiful girl to dance and she worries he's got two left feet.

Stefan rolled his eyes. "Yes, I can help with one arm."

Stefan's comment pierced through Elisabeth's anxiety and she laughed.

"I'm sorry," she said, her cheeks burning but Stefan

smiled back at her and she knew all was fine.

"Lissika!" Mammi called. "It's time to go!"

"Yes, Mammi!" Elisabeth said. Elisabeth now had an even bigger request to make of Mammi, so disobeying her right now was not going to help her win Mammi over. *But I know my request is the right thing for her.*

Georg and Samuel tipped their hats. "We should return, too," said Samuel. "It's not much longer that I'll be able to enjoy Mammi's cooking like my brother can!" He patted Georg on the back, a mischievous grin on his face. "He hates when I do that," he said as Georg narrowed his eyes. The two men began to head in the direction of their home, Samuel limping beside his big brother.

"Thank you," Eva said and hugged Elisabeth. "You've given me hope. Of all the boys and girls studying for confirmation, you are the most deserving one to pass." She squeezed her hands again and ran off to join her husband.

"That is high praise indeed," Stefan said. "And please, Elisabeth, don't hesitate to ask for help." He indicated toward his arm. "I need to find work to help my parents, but no one will hire me. I'm not asking for pay, but if people see me helping you, they may trust me to work for them." He smiled again and tipped his hat to her and Elisabeth blushed. As she ran to join Mammi, a new feeling arose in her, a giddiness that felt as though butterflies were fluttering all over her.

What did it mean?

CHAPTER SEVENTEEN

*J*uliana was snacking on a blueberry muffin before bed. After her talk with Mom and then dance class that evening, she was both famished and exhausted. But going to bed with a rumbling stomach rarely worked for her, so a late-night sugar boost it was.

The stairs squeaked as Opa came up. He smiled at Juliana and sat down. He inquired about school, and after Juliana told him about her marks, he produced a photo, without responding at all to her concerns. It was as though he already knew what he wanted to show her.

"I thought you might like to see this," he said. "I found it in the root cellar when I was looking for a shirt."

There was no way Opa would have found a shirt in the root cellar: Juliana had only been in there once, during

Christmas, and aside from dried bug carcasses, old mason jars, and boxes of old books—it was where she had found Omama's book of drawings—there was nothing. And certainly no clothing. *Another memory blip*, she thought glumly.

Juliana took the photo out of her hand and almost choked on a mouthful of muffin: it was a photo of a dead woman in a simple casket. An actual dead woman. Not a drawing, but a real photo. People stood behind the woman, their hands folded in prayer as they had in the drawing in Omama's book. Juliana now understood what Mom had meant, but as gross as the photo was, she couldn't keep her eyes off it: it was the first real photo she had seen of Opa's past. All the women had their heads covered, and the men wore their hair very short. *Almost like the Mennonites around here, but with a headscarf instead of a bonnet*, she thought.

The woman in the coffin wore a black kerchief and black clothing. The coffin looked almost more like a small bed on stick legs, with the body lying on white bedding, and a white blanket covering her up to her stomach. Her arms appeared tucked in at the sides and hidden under the blanket. Near the head of the coffin stood a sign similar to the one in the drawing.

"Who is that?" Juliana asked.

"I don't remember," Opa replied. "It says 'Susanna,' but I can't read her last name. I thought maybe it was my eyes. Can you read it?"

Juliana squinted as she tried to make out the letters. "It starts with an 'S,' and it's pretty long. Schuhmacher?"

Opa looked like he was running memories through his mind. "No. There's no Susanna Schuhmacher."

"It looks like...*S...c...h...u*...oh, that's a *b*, not an *h*."

"Schubkegel!"

Juliana broke out into laughter. She'd never heard such a funny name. "Shoop what?" she asked Opa.

"Schubkegel."

Juliana almost wanted to pretend she couldn't hear him, just to make him repeat himself again. But she didn't want him to think she was actually making fun of him.

He patted Juliana on the shoulder. "See? I knew it was my eyes."

Juliana studied the image a little harder. "Are these numbers when she was born and when she died?" She pointed to the years on the sign. "1903-1934?" Opa nodded. "So, who was she?"

"One of Mammi's cousins. This here is—"

"Wait!" Juliana cried and ran into her room to get her phone. "I want to record this!" It was already 10:30 at night, but whether her energy was from the sugar or this new information Opa had come to show her, she didn't know and she didn't care. She was just glad she had it. But this time she would video Opa. She remembered what Jasmine had said about his memory only getting worse, and she realized after the last time that not having video footage of a photo Opa described would make the explanation useless down the road. She just hoped he wouldn't object.

"Okay," she said as she returned and turned on her phone's video camera. "Do you mind?" At Opa's confused look, she explained what she wanted to do, without divulging that she had already recorded him before.

"That records video?" Opa pointed in amazement to her phone.

Juliana quickly explained how her phone worked and then pointed the camera at the photo so she could record. "You said this woman was Susanna...what was it again?"

"Schubkegel." This time Opa grinned too. He returned his attention to the photo and soon lost his smile. "This is Georg, Susi's brother. That he lived and she died...was unfair. He did nothing good for his family."

Opa was starting to sound like a constantly repeating commercial about this Georg but Juliana fought to stay quiet about it: she wanted the names in the photo. She zoomed in on Georg's face to get a close-up. "What was his last name?"

"Schuhmacher. My *opa* had a brother, Konrad. And Georg was one of his sons. Susanna was one of his daughters."

A lightbulb went off in Juliana's head. This had to be the same Susi in the drawing about the wedding. She wanted to ask Opa, but she feared distracting him from this photo.

"Hmm…I don't know this person." He pointed to a woman dressed eerily the same as the woman in the coffin, only she was standing and alive. She looked a lot younger than Georg, though it could have also been the photo. She was also smaller. "Oh! Of course," Opa said, as though a key in his mind had been found. "Eva. Georg's wife. She and Mammi were, I believe, very good friends."

It hadn't occurred to Juliana that her great-grandmother would have had friends. What did they talk about? Where did they hang out? Did they hang out? Or did they cook and clean all day? Wasn't that all that women did back then?

But so long as Opa's memory was flowing, she kept her mouth shut.

Opa pointed out Samuel and Gretche, the other two siblings in this branch of the Schuhmacher family, their spouses, and children.

"Where's Omama?" Juliana asked.

Opa smiled. "Probably behind the camera. She loved learning about new things."

Juliana was disappointed that she couldn't see a photo of her great-grandmother, so she moved on to her next observation. "I'm surprised the funeral home would have the body outside like this."

Opa burst out into laughter. "Oh no, Yulika. There were no funeral homes back then."

Juliana furrowed her eyebrows and she was almost

afraid to ask the next question. "Then...where did they keep them...?"

"In the home, of course."

"What?"

"When someone died, the family and friends cleared out most of the furniture in the back room, and the body was placed in there. When it was time to bury them, the coffin was closed and carried through the village to the cemetery. I can tell you more about it—"

"No, no, no, that's okay! I should probably get going to bed, anyways." Juliana glanced at the clock: 10:52.

"Of course. You have competition tomorrow in Toronto, don't you?"

Juliana nodded.

Opa smiled again, and Juliana could sense another memory coming through. Not sure whether Opa would let her video him directly, she switched to audio recording.

"I remember when your mother went to her first dance competition. She was maybe eleven or twelve. She had this costume on..." He shook his head and laughed. "She was supposed to be like some kind of toy...a stuffed toy that turned into a pillow or something."

"Huh?"

"I know there's a picture around here somewhere." Then he glanced at Juliana. "But she probably wouldn't want you to see it: it really embarrassed her." Then he giggled. "*Sie war so niedlich!*" Juliana didn't understand him, but he didn't stop to explain. Judging by his intonation, it was something nice. "Well, I need my sleep so I can pack tomorrow. I leave Saturday for Cuba, but we'll see each other tomorrow morning before you go. Good night!"

Juliana asked if she could keep the photo of Susanna. Opa nodded. "You're so organized you'll make sure it doesn't get lost. Wait."

Juliana was worried he would take the photo back.

"Katy's birthday is soon, isn't it?" He walked over to the calendar hanging on the wall in the kitchen, beside the television, and flipped to the next month. "Yes, there it is," he said, stabbing the date with his finger a few times. "We should have a little party for her. I'll talk to Anne when she drives me and Karl to the airport on Saturday. I should call Peter, too."

Opa headed downstairs without saying another word, leaving Juliana with the photo of her deceased ancestor. She took the photo to her room so she could compare it with the drawing in Omama's book.

The picture didn't gross her out as much anymore. In fact, the more she learned about Omama's family and friends, the more questions she had, and the more she hoped photos like this one would help her. Juliana was only now starting to get to know her cousins, whereas her great-grandmother had obviously grown up with hers. How big was her family? Were they her friends? What other friends did she have? What did they do? She couldn't imagine them having sleepovers like she and Rachel had had, but what did she know? Maybe they did. Did they eat chocolate until they almost got sick? Or make popcorn? Or watch movies? Or colour each other's hair? *Well, if they didn't have electricity, then I guess movies are out*, she thought, laughing at herself.

Juliana sat down on her bed and pulled Omama's book out of her nightstand. She tucked in her earbuds and replayed the video she had just taken of Opa. As he said the name on each photo, Juliana pointed to each one in the drawing of the funeral. Worried she'd forget the names, she took out of her desk a notebook that she had started to record her research about Opa's family and drew a mock-up of the drawing, muttering to herself how she clearly hadn't inherited this artistic gene. She replayed the video a few more times as she wrote the names down, doing her best with the spelling. "Georg" she knew from *The Sound of Music*, but "Ayfa"? She did the best she could with all of them and promised herself she'd ask Mom when they got back from competition.

Juliana yawned. It was well past her bedtime. She quickly changed into pyjamas and slipped under the covers.

But she lay awake thinking about photos. Where would she be without them? No matter what happened between her and Rachel now, Juliana would always have her photos of the two of them, and if she missed Rachel but couldn't reach her, she could at least see her in any of hundreds, maybe even thousands of photos that Juliana had, or go online and see what Rachel was posting on her social media accounts.

Opa had this single photo of a funeral. Juliana knew Opa hadn't grown up with this technology. Heck, Dad had once said he didn't even have the Internet until he was in his teens. So if they couldn't take a million photos...*They would only take photos of the really important things*, she thought. Suddenly, this picture of a deceased cousin was beautiful: this Susanna must have been loved.

Mom had mentioned that Opa had received several photos of funerals. And that photo of Mom sounded too irresistible to leave buried somewhere. But where would Juliana start looking? In the wall unit in the living room? Or in that bug-carcass-infested root cellar? That was where Opa had found this photo. She knew an encyclopedia set was in those boxes, but she didn't know what else was down there.

"When I get back," she said to herself, "I'm going to find those pictures." Then she thought about her upcoming time commitments: catching up on homework next week, dance class, practice...But she knew she would somehow make it work.

"I'll have something fun to tell Rachel about when we talk," she thought to herself. "Or maybe I'll even write her a letter."

SETTING THE RECORD STRAIGHT

Between Worlds tells a fictional contemporary story together with a story that is historical fiction. In both parts of the book, I've taken facts about life in that time and included them in a fictional story. In writing novels, the story always comes first (because otherwise this would be a history text-book), so this section explains any facts that may have been changed to fit the story, and adds some more background to the story. If you have any questions about what you've read in this or any of the other books in the series, ask away! My contact information is in the "Stay in Touch!" section.

GRADE 9 GEOGRAPHY

Certainly one of the biggest differences between Juliana and Elisabeth is that Juliana is in grade nine while Elisabeth finished school after grade six. For Juliana's geography lessons, I'm following the textbook used in Ontario high schools, *Making Connections, 3rd edition ON, Student Annual Subscription STU*, published by Pearson Canada.

USING KITCHENER BUSINESSES AND SITES

Juliana's life takes place in Kitchener, Ontario. She lives near Grand River Hospital, one of the two hospitals in the city. In this book, I introduced Belmont Village, a collection of shops, restaurants, and other businesses along a stretch of Belmont Avenue near her home. I lived in this neighbourhood for a few years in my teens and loved going to Belmont Village to grab the latest *Superman* comic or to pick up something from the drug store or health food store. In this series, although Belmont Village does exist, any businesses are fictional. (If you've ever been to any of the businesses there, though, give them a shout-out on my Facebook page. I'm sure they'd appreciate it.)

NEWS IN SEMLAK

News in Semlak was delivered once a week by the postman, who would indeed beat his drum to gather people around him and shout out the week's headlines. All headlines used in this book were discovered by my translator, Gabriela Rat, in Romania. She found digitized copies of *Românul*, a daily newspaper from Arad, the main city in Arad County, which Semlak belonged to. The headlines in this book are from the issues dated February 27, March 6, and March 11, 1920. If you read Romanian, you can read the newspaper here: http://dspace.bcucluj.ro/handle/123456789/15738.

LUTHER'S CATECHISM

Martin Luther wrote two catechisms, appropriately titled in English *The Large Catechism* and *The Small Catechism*. The small one was meant for laypeople and families, and it's this that Elisabeth is studying. It explains to worshippers what important parts of the Bible mean. This is a cornerstone of the Lutheran faith because Martin Luther believed that Christianity had moved too far away from the Bible. For this reason, he translated the Christian holy book into German so laypeople could read it (if they were literate, which wasn't assured in the 16th century). If you'd like to read more about Luther's *Small Catechism*, visit https://catechism.cph.org. For this series, though, I used the following source: *A Short Exposition of Dr. Martin Luther's Small Catechism*, published in 1905 by Concordia Publishing House in St. Louis, Missouri. This gave me religious language closer to what Elisabeth would have read could she read English. This version is an authorized translation by the Evangelical Lutheran Synodical Conference of North America.

One other point I should explain is the Ten Commandments. Elisabeth keeps referring to "honour thy father and thy mother" as the fourth commandment. You may know it as the fifth commandment. Neither is right or wrong, but Christian denominations count the Ten Commandments differently.

CONFIRMATION

Confirmation is essentially an initiation ritual, after which children in the Lutheran church are considered adults. In Semlak, this traditionally happened on Palm Sunday, the Sunday before Easter.

In the Lutheran church in Semlak, confirmed but unmarried teenagers were called *großbuben* and *großmädchen*. This translates directly as *big boys* and *big girls*. Because we associate those terms with little kids, like when we say, "Oh my! What a big boy you are now!" after a three-year-old shows you his muscles, I chose to keep the German terms.

THE LUTHERAN CHURCH

If you'd like to get a better look at Semlak's Lutheran church, you can visit http://www.semlak.de/en/picture-gallery/churches/the-protestant-church.html to see relatively recent photos of it. You can also see a recent ecumenical Christmas service taking place here: https://youtu.be/sulbqzCEj7g. Remember, the church in Elisabeth's time had no electricity, so I don't know at this point if the chandeliers once held candles, or whether light was produced a different way.

SEATING RULES IN SEMLAK'S LUTHERAN CHURCH

If I waited to start this series until I completed all necessary research, I'd be retired before I could release the first book. These stories felt too important to hold on to for that long.

One change I needed to make to the series was the seating in Elisabeth's church: I only learned recently that it was more regimented than I had originally known for *Between Worlds 1: The Move*. Although the series is fiction, I believe details like this highlight just how different this society was from Juliana's and our own. For example, after teenagers were confirmed in Elisabeth's church, they actually sat separately from their younger siblings and cousins, but the fact that they were not allowed to sit with the married and widowed adults suggests that they weren't considered to be adults in society. I chose to make the change in this book so I can continue with this hierarchy in subsequent books.

REAL PEOPLE IN SEMLAK

These novels are fiction, and aside from historical figures, most characters are also fictional. This gives me more freedom to work with their personalities, and I don't risk offending someone's memory by making things up. However, Pastor Fröhlich did indeed exist. I felt that including the real pastor of the community would help anchor it in history, and he struck me as someone readers might find interesting down the road.

I know little about his true personality, other than that he was a controversial figure in Semlak. For example, after Semlak transferred to Romania, he wanted to continue the church's connection to a church synod (association of churches) in Hungary. However, most in the congregation wanted to join the Lutheran synod in Hermannstadt, Romania. In addition, in July 1920, the church received the directive that its schools should teach in German, but Pastor Fröhlich refused. When *Between Worlds* comes to this point in Elisabeth's story, I'll likely delve into this issue more.

As for Pastor Fröhlich's take on Georg's post-traumatic

stress disorder, I can only guess. This is an example of the story coming first in historical fiction.

GALICIA

Although there is a Galicia in Spain, the Galicia referred to in this series is a historical region that straddles Central and Eastern Europe. It once belonged to the Austrian-Hungarian Empire. Many battles in World War I were fought here. You can read the Wikipedia entry on Galicia for more information: https://en.wikipedia.org/wiki/Galicia_(Eastern_Europe)

POST-TRAUMATIC STRESS DISORDER

PTSD is a diagnosable mental illness whose label in English during and, for a time, after World War I was often "shell shock." Its existence has been known for centuries, but under different names. Because of the scale of World War I, it began to garner more attention.

However, unlike Georg and thousands more like him in his time, we understand it better today. For example, did you know that early theories of this illness suggested that men were losing their masculinity? Moreover, some doctors believed that the amount of "maleness" a man received at birth would determine if he was strong enough to withstand war. A really interesting article on this topic was written by Jessica Meyer: "Separating the Men from the Boys: Masculinity and Maturity in Understandings of Shell Shock in Britain," published in *Twentieth Century British History*, volume 20, No. 1, 2009, pages 1-22.

PTSD has a range of symptoms. Georg's case is severe but certainly not representative of what every soldier deals with. For a reliable introduction on the subject, visit this website: https://www.veterans.gc.ca/eng/health-support/mental-health-and-wellness/understanding-mental-health/ptsd-warstress.

For a ten-minute video introduction on shell shock specifically, visit *The Great War* YouTube channel. (Note that some scenes may be disturbing to some viewers): https://youtu.be/kvTRJZGWqF8

STAY IN TOUCH!

If you enjoyed the book, sign up for my monthly newsletter! I write it myself, so it's my words to you. You'll get the following:

- Sneak peeks at upcoming books
- Updates about online and in-person appearances
- Book and writing recommendations
- Recipes I love
- Contests
- And more!

Visit BetweenWorldsYA.com to sign up!

Prefer social media? All my links are listed under my bio, at the end of the book.

ACKNOWLEDGEMENTS

Thank you to the following people for their continued encouragement: Mom & Dad, Kristin, Deardra (my former dance teacher), and The Straus Haus (hubby Corey, and my two kids, Khristopher and Jonnathan).

Again my thanks to Gabriela Rat, who researched and translated the newspaper headlines used in the book; to Georg Schmidt of the HOG Semlak; and to DVHH.org.

It has again been a pleasure in working with my editing team: Heather Wright (writing coach and consulting editor) and Susan Fish (editor). They helped me find the right touch in writing a book that dealt with a very personal subject and that also explored a very serious condition and how people can perceive it. I'm also indebted to Michelle Fairbanks of Fresh Design, my graphics designer, whose patience helped us find the gorgeous photo for this book; and to Ali MacGee, for her writerly advice and mentorship.

ABOUT LORI

Photo by Erin Watt Photography

Lori Wolf-Heffner is a former competitive dancer, dance teacher, and theatre manager. She was a member of the first Canadian National Tap Team, back in 1996, under the leadership of Bonnie Dyer, with choreographer Mathew Clark. She's written for *Dance Canada Quarterly*, *just dance!* magazine, and *The Dance Current* (all under Lori Straus).

Fluent in German, Lori lived in Germany for three years, never once realizing just how close she was to some of the villages her ancestors left to migrate to Eastern Europe in the 1700s.

Lori lives in Waterloo, Ontario, Canada, with her husband and two sons. She is a member of The Writers' Union of Canada and the Alliance of Independent Authors.

facebook.com/loriwolfheffner

x.com/LoriWolfHeffner

instagram.com/loriwolfheffner

goodreads.com/lori_wolf-heffner

bookbub.com/author/lori-wolf-heffner

pinterest.com/loriwolfheffner

amazon.com/author/loriwolfheffner